DANA'S HOMECOMING

PART II

NEW BEGINNINGS

Angela D. Evans

authorHOUSE®

AuthorHouse™
1663 Liberty Drive
Bloomington, IN 47403
www.authorhouse.com
Phone: 1-800-839-8640

First published by AuthorHouse 04/19/2011

ISBN: 978-1-4567-6939-0 (sc)
ISBN: 978-1-4567-6938-3 (e)

Printed in the United States of America

Chapter One
The Reunion

Maurice held Dana in his arms. Dana could sense that he had missed her. He turned her toward him and asked, "Dana, do you know how much I missed you?"

Dana replied, "No. How much did you miss me?"

Maurice said with a low voice, "More than you'll ever know."

"I missed you too."

"Why didn't you tell me that you were coming home?"

"I didn't want you to rush your business trip. I figured it had to be important if you were going to be away that long."

"It was important, but I only went because I couldn't bear being in this house without you."

"I'm sorry."

"Don't be. I shouldn't have suggested that you go. Don't ever leave me again."

"Although I missed you terribly, I think it did me good to go. I did a lot of thinking and cleared my head. I'll never leave you again." Dana kissed Maurice.

Maurice asked, "Well what are your plans now that you're back?"

"I'm returning to work. I'm going back to take my position at the clinic."

"I know everyone will be happy."

"I hope so. I called last week and told them that I'll return next month. I also would like us to try for that extended family."

With a mischievous look in his eyes, Maurice pulled Dana closer to him. He teased her lips and then kissed her with such passion it left her mind whirling. Their passion rose to heights unimaginable. They fell asleep clinging to each other, not wanting to be apart. At twelve in the afternoon, Maurice woke up and eased out of bed. He called the hospital and told them that he would not be returning to work for three weeks. He then showered and dressed in lounging clothes. He went downstairs to the kitchen. He made lunch for the two of them. Along with the lunch, he mixed fresh strawberries, blueberries, and cantaloupe in a bowl. He carried Cool Whip with him. Before going upstairs, he called the florist and ordered two dozen multi-colored roses. When he entered the room, Dana was waking up. She looked around and then spotted him walking into the room. She smiled.

Dana said, "You are so sweet."

Maurice responded, "I know. Remember that."

He placed the food on a serving table. Dana got out of bed.

She said, "I'm going to take a shower."

"Don't be too long."

"I won't."

While Dana was in the shower, the doorbell rang. Maurice went to answer it. It was the florist. He tipped the delivery person and thanked him. Maurice returned to their bedroom with the flowers. He placed them on the dresser. He made up the bed. When Dana came out of the bathroom, she was dressed in a pale pink lounging pant set. As she looked at Maurice and saw the desire in his eyes, she turned red from blushing. She couldn't believe how he was making her feel. As she walked toward Maurice, Dana noticed the flowers.

"Maurice, they are beautiful."

"Just like you."

"When did you get them?"

"While you were asleep."

Dana kissed him and then sat down.

As Maurice kissed Dana, he said, "Don't start anything."

"I'm not. I just wanted to thank you."

"We'll take care of that later."

Maurice smiled. He served Dana the food. After they had eaten their meal, Maurice opened the Cool Whip and spread it over the fruit. He fed her the fruit. She then picked up a strawberry and fed it to him. After they were full, Maurice turned on music.

Maurice took her hand and asked, "May I have this dance?"

She replied, "Of course."

She rose to her feet. He drew her in close. They swayed to the music. As the song's played, they were swept away. Dana thought, *How good it feels being in his arms.* She felt safe. Maurice lifted her face to look at him.

Maurice whispered, "I love you. You are so beautiful. When I look at you and I am close to you, I feel complete. Those two years that you refused to love me were the saddest time in my life; you see, when you meet your soul mate and you're kept from them, you can't be complete. You feel empty. Then you went away, not just out of the state, but you closed yourself away from me and left me all alone. That's why I had to get out of this house. Don't ever leave me again."

"I won't. I wanted so much to make you as happy as you made me. You made me face my fear, and I will always love you for that. I didn't realize until I returned home that this is where I am supposed to be."

Maurice bent down and kissed her. He held her with such a way that she could feel him tremble. Dana returned his embrace. The music played on as they made love. The two lay in each other's arms, not wanting the moment to end. For the next two weeks, the couple was inseparable. They talked of their future and having children. To Maurice's surprise, he did not see sadness in Dana's eyes, nor did he feel uncomfortable discussing the possibility of her becoming pregnant. As it got closer to them returning to work, sadness came over Dana. She enjoyed them being in their own little world.

September came, and they both returned to work. Maurice made his rounds, and Dana reacquainted herself with the clinic. Everyone was ecstatic about her return. Dana saw a few patients. As the months rolled by, Dana was feeling sick. She saw her doctor, but it was not what she expected. The doctor told her that she was overworked and that she needed to slow down. Dana's illness years before had weakened her heart. Dana did as she was told. She cut back her late nights and decided that she would work three days a week rather than five. Maurice cut his hours as well. The couple tried to spend as much time together as possible. The couple realized that their strength was from being with each other.

When December came, Dana and Maurice decided to take off a week and visit her parents in Mobile, Alabama. They took an early flight out. When they arrived at Dana's mother's home, there wasn't anyone home. The house was decorated as always, but Dana could feel something was wrong. They drove to Mary's house. When they arrived, Tom answered the door. He told them that Mary had gone to the hospital to meet her mother because their father had just been rushed to Mobile Infirmary. Dana thanked Tom for the information. She and Maurice went to Mobile Infirmary. When they arrived in the emergency room, Mary was sitting in the waiting area crying.

Dana rushed to her side and held her. Mary looked in disbelief that Dana was there. She wiped her eyes.

Mary said, "What are you doing here?"

Dana responded, "We came to spend Christmas with you guys."

Mary asked, "How did you know to come here?"

"We went to Mom's and no one was there. Then we went to your house. Tom told us that you were here with Mom and Dad."

"Dad had a heart attack. He's not doing too well."

Maurice said, "I'll talk to the doctor. I'll see what information I can get. I know some people on the board here."

Maurice kissed both women on the forehead. He went over to the nurses' station. Within minutes, a tall, fiftyish man came to meet him. They shook hands and then disappeared through a set of doors. They were gone for twenty minutes. When they emerged, Dana stood up. Maurice and the doctor walked over to Dana and Mary. Maurice introduced the doctor as Dr. Walker, chief of staff. Dr. Walker greeted both ladies and then explained what had happened to their father. He explained how they planned to treat him. When Christmas came, everyone tried to appear cheerful, but it wasn't the same. Everyone opened their gifts. They ate breakfast. A few times they talked about and laughed at their memories of past Christmases with their father being there. After some time, everyone dressed and then headed to the hospital with gifts for their father. When they arrived at the hospital, the doctor was at the nurses' station.

He said, "Merry Christmas."

Mrs. Carrington said, "Merry Christmas."

The doctor said, "I have good news for you. Come into my office."

The group followed the doctor.

He said, "Have a seat. I know I said that Mr. Carrington would be here another week, but because of his last test results, I feel that he is strong enough to go home today."

The group all looked at each other in disbelief.

Mrs. Carrington asked, "Are you sure?"

The doctor answered, "Yes. He needs a lot of rest. I'll give you his prescriptions. Make sure he takes it as prescribed."

"I will, Doctor."

The doctor asked, "Do you have any questions?"

Mrs. Carrington answered, "No."

They left the doctor's office and headed toward Mr. Carrington's room. They entered his room. Everyone took their time hugging and greeting Mr. Carrington.

Mr. Carrington asked, "Did the doctor tell you that I can go home today?"

Mrs. Carrington replied, "Yes."

Dana said, "Maurice and I will leave now. We'll go put the prescriptions in."

Mrs. Carrington said, "Good. We'll meet you back at the house."

Dana kissed her parents. She and Maurice left. They drove to nearest drug store and put the prescriptions in. The drug store was centered in one of the historic areas of Mobile. The couple decided to walk around the area to view some of the sights while they wait. Hand in hand Maurice and Dana looked at the beautiful old homes. Dana marveled at how beautiful they were. Dana loved the way they used to make the homes with the high posts outside of the home. She felt that these homes were built with such care and the workers took pride in their work. After an hour, Dana and Maurice returned to the drug store. The prescriptions were ready. When they arrived at her mother's home, everyone was already there. Her father was seated in his favorite seat. He was smiling broader then she had ever remembered. As it began to get late, Maurice walked over to Mr.

Carrington and said, "I don't mean to break up the party, but Dad needs to get some rest."

With that everyone hugged Mr. Carrington. Maurice helped him into the guest bedroom, which was located on the first level of the house. He checked his vitals and gave Mr. Carrington his heart medication. Mr. Carrington fell asleep soon after Maurice left the room. Within an hour, everyone began to leave.

Dana and Maurice stayed a week longer than they planned. When that week ended, Dana and Maurice packed and brought their luggage to the foyer.

Dana asked, "Mom, are you sure you'll be okay?"

Mrs. Carrington answered, "We will be fine. Thank you both for staying as long as you have, but you need to get back."

Mrs. Carrington kissed them both. They went into their father's room. They both kissed him and said, "Make sure you rest and take your medicine."

The two left for the airport. They returned their vehicle and headed for the boarding gate. Once on the plane, the two fell asleep before the plane had taken off. When they awakened, the plane was landing.

Dana said, "I didn't realize I was so tired."

Maurice said, "Me either."

They exited the plane and headed for baggage. Once Maurice and Dana got their luggage, they took the airport taxi to their car. Once in the car, Dana fell asleep again. When they arrived home, Maurice told Dana to lie down. She showered and then slipped on some lounging wear and got into bed. Maurice brought the luggage into the house. He carried it upstairs to their bedroom. Before putting it away, he went over to Dana and felt her forehead. She wasn't warm. He kissed her forehead and then proceeded to put their clothes away. He then went down to the kitchen and cooked dinner. When he was done, he carried the meal up to their room. He woke Dana up.

She smiled and said, "You are such a good husband. What time is it?"

"Six."

"I slept that long?"

"Yes. Are you feeling okay?"

"I'm fine. I'm just a little tired. We've had a busy two weeks."

"I know, but I still think that you should call your doctor and get a check up."

Dana knew he was concerned, so she did not argue. After dinner Maurice cleaned up the kitchen and put up the dishes. Dana went through the mail and wrote out checks for the bills. Dana and Maurice decided to go to bed early. Maurice held her all night. They didn't awaken until nine o'clock the next morning. Dana and Maurice got out of bed and showered together. After Dana was dressed, she called her doctor. To her surprise, Dana was able to get an appointment at twelve. Maurice drove her to the doctor. When she arrived at the doctor's office, Dana signed in. A few minutes later, she was called. Dana and Maurice were escorted to an examining room. The nurse took her vitals. After they waited fifteen minutes, the doctor entered the room. He asked Dana her reason for being there. The doctor ordered blood work to be done and for Dana to submit to a urine test. The nurse performed the task of drawing Dana's blood. Dana was given a cup. After returning to the room, the doctor checked her vitals again and told her to lay back. He turned on the monitor and ran the scope over Dana's stomach. As he looked, the nurse came into the room with Dana's results. The doctor read the results. He did not say anything. The doctor returned his attention to the monitor. He saw an image.

The doctor said, "Well, it looks like congratulations are in order."

Maurice looked at Dana and then at the doctor. He said, "Are you saying what I think you're saying?"

"Yes, you are going to have a baby."

With tears in her eyes, Dana looked at the doctor. Dana didn't believe what she was hearing. Dana asked, "Are you sure?"

The doctor said, "Well let's see, your blood test and urinalysis are positive and do you see that little speck there? That's your baby, so yes, I am sure you are pregnant."

Dana sat up and hugged the doctor. She said, "I'm sorry, but I didn't think that I would ever hear those words."

The doctor said, "Well you are. Here is a prescription for prenatal vitamins."

Maurice's excitement turned to worry. He asked, "Doctor, will this affect her heart?"

"With rest she should be fine. We will keep a close watch, and I will schedule the delivery, so there will be as little stress as possible."

"Should she go on bed rest now?"

"Dana, I'm not going to put you out of work yet. Make sure you take your vitamins every day, and I want you to not work too hard. Come back to see me in a month. We'll see how you're doing then."

The doctor walked out of the room. Dana dressed. She looked at Maurice with tears streaming down her face. He hugged her. Dana could tell that he was holding back his emotions. As they walked out of the room, the couple gleamed with pride. Dana made an appointment, and they left the office. Maurice drove to the drug store and put in Dana's prescription. After receiving the vitamins, Maurice drove Dana home. He dropped her off at their home and told her that he was going grocery shopping. He wanted to make sure that Dana had a healthy pregnancy. Dana was so proud to be pregnant and happy that Maurice would help her to stay on track. Although she was thrilled by the doctor's news Dana wanted to keep her pregnancy quiet until she was further along.

Two hours later, Maurice returned home. He carried the groceries in. Dana was still awake. She was too excited to rest. After Maurice had put up the food, he started upstairs. He found Dana in the room that was going to be the baby room. She was just standing there. Maurice up from behind her and placed his arms around her waist. Maurice said, "Isn't it wonderful?"

"Yes it is. I'm going to be a mom."

Maurice rubbed Dana's stomach. "I knew we would be blessed one way or another. You are too good a person and have so much to give not to have a baby."

Dana cut her hours at work. She wanted to make sure that she did not overdo it. Dana didn't want to lose this baby. Dana had come so far and didn't know whether she could survive another setback.

Chapter Two
The Pregnancy

A month had gone by, and Dana was excited to see the doctor. When Dana returned to the doctor, she was told that she was five months pregnant. She was able to hear the baby's heartbeat. Dana couldn't contain the tears that streamed down her eyes. She was so happy. That night while lying in the bed, she felt the baby move. Dana called out to Maurice. He came into the room. Dana took his hand and placed it on her stomach. After a few minutes, the baby kicked. Maurice couldn't believe how wonderful it felt.

Maurice asked, "Does it hurt?"

"No. It feels wonderful. I heard the heartbeat today. It was so clear."

"I'll go with you next time."

During the next two months, Dana decided to do one full day at the clinic. Dana was now seven months pregnant. She decided to tell her staff. She called Rita. Rita was very happy for her. Rita offered to babysit and help out in any way she could. Dana was happy to hear that Rita's family was doing well. They were in the process of buying a house. The twins were now in kindergarten. The next day, Marsha called Dana.

When Dana answered the phone, Marsha said, "Hey, girl. I heard. Why didn't you call me? Girl, I saw your mother in the grocery store two days ago and she said that you were pregnant."

"Yes I am. I wanted to get through a few months before I told anyone."

"Okay, I forgive you. So how many months are you?"

"I'm going into my eighth month."

"Wow. I am so happy for you. Do you know what you're having?"

"No, we wanted to be surprised."

"Well, you better call me when you have the baby."

"Of course I will."

"So I guess you're waiting to have the shower?"

"Yes. I'll let you know."

"What are you doing these days?"

"Going out of my mind. I'm not working now, and I'm trying not to buy anything. I read to the baby and watch TV. I'm not allowed to do much more."

"Your doctor really got you on a strict bed rest."

"Yes, my doctor husband. He's sweet though."

"Oh, that's so nice. Well, I'm not going to keep you any longer."

"I'll call you soon."

"Okay. It was nice talking to you. Love you."

When Dana was in her ninth month, she began to have contractions. The doctor did what she could to stop the contractions. In the second week of her ninth month, the doctor scheduled Dana for delivery. Maurice packed Dana's bag, and they left for the hospital. By nine o'clock, Dana had been prepared and delivered by eleven o'clock. She gave birth to a five-pound, five-ounce baby boy. They named him after Maurice. Maurice was beside himself. As he held the baby, tears streamed down his face. He kissed his son. Dana smiled, and her eyes filled with tears as she saw how proud Maurice was. After three days, the family was able to go home. To Dana's surprise, the baby's room had been furnished. Maurice had someone come in while she was in the hospital. She marveled at the precise detail that had been replicated from their conversations on how she had envisioned the room.

Dana said with tears flowing down her face, "This is beautiful. How did you do this so fast?"

"I had help."

After a week had gone by, Dana's mother and father came up. Maurice picked them up at the airport. When Dana went downstairs, her parents, Mary, and her family were there. A few days later they surprised Dana with a baby shower. Marsha called her during the shower. She had sent a gift up by Mary. After the shower was over and everyone had gone, Dana went up to her room. Her mother, Mary, and Karen followed her. Dana's father went to lie down. Maurice, Tom, and Dave began cleaning up. After they were done, the men went into the family room, turned on the television, and watched sports. After Dave and Karen left, the group broke up. Mary took Tom by the hand and led him to the guest room to go to bed. Dana's mother said good night to everyone and joined her husband. Maurice went up to their room. He showered, went in to check on the baby, and then returned to their bedroom.

Dana said, "I can't believe you."

"What?"

"How did you manage to pull all of this off?"

He got into bed, pulled her close, and then said, "It wasn't hard. Everyone thinks so much of you that I had to turn some help down. You know you are such a good person that people are thrilled to do anything for you."

They laid basking in the quiet, happy to be alone together. Just then the baby began to cry.

Maurice said, "I'll get Alex."

By the time he had gotten up and entered the baby's room, Mrs. Carrington had already picked Alex up.

She said, "Go rest. I'll feed my grandson."

"Okay. Let me know if you need anything."

"I will. Good night."

"Good night."

Maurice left the baby's room and went back into his bedroom. He got in bed and pulled Dana close to him.

Dana said, "Where's Alex?"

"Mom has him."

"That woman is always busy."

They kissed and then fell asleep.

Dana and Maurice were thrilled that the family was there helping out, but they were equally excited two weeks later when the family's visit came to an end. The couple wanted to be alone with their new baby. The families said their good-byes. Maurice drove them to the airport.

Chapter Three
Dana Return's to Work

As time passed, Dana returned to work. Dana awakened, showered, and got ready for work. When she arrived at work, Dana entered the office and began getting the office ready for clients. When she opened the clinic doors, a young girl came in.

Dana asked, "Can I help you?"

She answered, "Yes ma'am. I'm pregnant and I don't know what to do."

"Where are your parents?"

"I only have a mother."

"Where is she?"

"She's at home."

"Have you told her about the baby?"

"No ma'am."

"Why not."

"I'm afraid. You see, my mother had great hopes for me. I don't want to disappoint her."

"I don't think you can disappoint her."

"I was supposed to be a dancer."

"You can still be a dancer."

"Not with a baby. If I have the baby, I have to give up my dreams."

"Not necessarily. Maybe you can get someone to help, like the father."

"That's a joke." She began to cry.

Dana handed her a Kleenex.

"As soon as I told him that I thought I was pregnant, he asked who the father was. He was my first, and it was my first time. We used protection, but first he wanted to feel me so we put on the condom later."

"Well let's just give you a test and then we'll go from there. I will need you to fill out a form; it's just one page to get a little information from you."

"You won't tell anyone, will you?"

"I'm your doctor. I can only tell if you give me permission."

"Good. I was scared. My mother always told me you were a good lady."

Dana's hair stood up on her arms. She didn't want to ask who this girl's mother was, because she didn't want to alarm the girl. Dana figured that she would find out after the girl filled out the form. The young girl completed the form and handed it back to Dana. Dana read the name: Rashonda Greene. Dana thought to herself, *I don't remember a Greene. This child is fifteen years old. I have to convince her to talk to her mother, whoever she is.* Dana handed Rashonda a cup. "Please pee in this cup and put it in the window of the bathroom. Then come back."

Rashonda said, "Okay."

Rashonda did as she was told. When she returned to Dana's office, they talked more about the potential father. Rashonda explained, "He is seventeen. He is getting ready to graduate. I thought that he loved me and that I was going to go to his prom. But the way he's acting I don't want to talk to him." She began to cry again. "I thought he loved me. I really messed up. What am I going to do? I saw him with this fast girl on the way over here. They saw me and began to laugh."

Just then a nurse's assistant came into the office with the results.

The assistant handed the results to Dana. She said, "Here, Dr. Carrington."

"Thanks, Margaret."

When the assistant left the office, Dana read the results. She was hoping that it was negative. Dana said, "Your test is positive. You really need to discuss this with your mother. If you like, I can be with you when you tell her or I can tell her."

"Would you? I mean tell her. I'll bring her tomorrow. Is that okay?"

"That would be great. You need to make whatever decision you are going to make as soon as possible."

"Well, Doctor, I'll come back at two. Is that all right?"

"Yes, I'll see you tomorrow at two."

The next day Dana couldn't help being anxious about Rashonda's visit. She could not imagine who her mother was. Two o'clock came, but there was no sign of Rashonda. Two-thirty came and went. Dana became worried that Rashonda would be another teenager waiting until it's too late to get medical care or even worse, do something desperate when they don't know how their parents will react. At three o'clock two days later, Rashonda showed up at the clinic with her mother. It was evident that she had not told her mother of her condition. When Dana came out of her office she, Rashonda's mother was seated in the waiting area. Dana recognized her mother to be Ms. Brown. She went over to greet them.

Dana said, "Hi, Ms. Brown. How are you?"

"I was fine until my child informed me that she needed me to come down to the clinic. What is this about?" Turning to Rashonda, she said, "I told you I didn't want you to get on birth control. You should be thinking about dancing."

"Momma, please."

Dana interrupted, "Please come into my office where we can have some privacy."

Ms. Brown got up. "I don't care where we go, I'm not signing anything to get her birth control." She looked at Rashonda. "I can't believe you dragged me down here for this. You see how I'm struggling with you and your sisters and brother by myself. You can wait to have sex. Those little boys don't know what they're doing anyway. I want more for you. Look at me. I had sex when I was your age and look where it got me."

"Ms. Brown, please. Just listen. Your daughter didn't bring you here to get birth control. She needs you to listen and help her to make a very important decision."

"What decision?"

"Rashonda is pregnant."

Ms. Brown looked at Dana in disbelief. She then turned to Rashonda with a look of hurt and disappointment. As she walked out of Dana's office, she said, "I don't believe you. You've seen how hard it's been for us since your father left. The only money we get from him is when child support takes his taxes. You see how hard it is for me to raise you and your brothers and sisters. I can't raise another."

Ms. Brown left out of the office.

Dana looked at Rashonda and said, "Stay here, I'll go talk to her."

Rashonda sat as if frozen. She had tears streaming down her face. Dana followed Ms. Brown. She caught up to her and said, "Ms. Brown, please wait. I understand you're upset."

"Upset? I'm not upset. I'm angry that I've tried to raise my girls not to end up like me and the one child that I thought would end up doing something with her life follows right behind me. I thought at least she was listening. I cannot believe this. And now what am I supposed to do? Raise a grandchild? My youngest is five. I thought I was done with changing diapers and now I'm expected to start over? Now she got to quit school and go to work. I can't afford another mouth to feed. I guess the snot-nosed boy dumped her."

"Ms. Brown, Rashonda needs you. This is not the time to abandon her. She has no one but you. Yes, it would have been nice if this didn't happen, but it did and she needs you to help her deal with this. She still can obtain her dreams. It's just going to take more work. There are programs that can help. Please come back to my office so we can discuss this with your daughter."

Ms. Brown followed Dana back to her office. When they entered the office, Rashonda was seated with her head in her hands. When she heard the door, she lifted her head and tried to wipe away the tears.

Rashonda said, "Mom, I'm sorry. I'll get an abortion and then everything will be okay. I promise I will go to school and get good grades. And I'll study dancing better than before. I won't let any boy touch me no more."

Hearing this made Ms. Brown sad. She looked at Dana with such regret that Dana walked over to her, bent down, and said, "Tell your daughter how you really feel."

Ms. Brown looked at Rashonda and said, "Baby, I love you. I just want the best for you. I don't want you, your sisters, or your brother to struggle like I had to. I didn't have a chance to be a kid, and I wanted you to enjoy life, to meet someone who would love you as much as you love him. Do you want to have this baby?"

"I loved Peter, but he just used me. It hurts." Rashonda began to cry. "When I realized I was pregnant, I was scared, but I was happy too, because I thought me and Peter was in love. I wanted to have this baby. Mom, it was my first time. I never let anyone touch me before. I thought we would get married. I can't believe I was so wrong. I don't know what to do. I already love the baby. Is that stupid?"

Dana said, "No, but you have to make a decision quickly. You are two months, and if you decide not to have the baby, we have to take care of this before it's too late."

Ms. Brown said, "Baby, I'm here for you no matter what you decide. Things are going to be tight if you decide to have this baby. I know this decision is hard, and whatever you decide, you have to be able to live with it."

Rashonda sat for a few minutes. She looked at her mother and then closed her eyes. She kept them closed for ten minutes before opening them and saying, "I want to keep the baby." Tears rolled down her face. Ms. Brown moved closer to her daughter. She hugged her. They held each other as both cried. Dana's eyes filled with tears.

Dana reached over to get tissue. After wiping her eyes, she said, "Am I correct to say that you're going through with the pregnancy?"

Rashonda wiped her eyes and said, "Yes."

Dana said, "I'll write you a prescription for prenatal vitamins. Make sure you take them every day. I would like to see you back in a month."

Rashonda walked over to Dana, gave her a hug, and said, "Thank you. My mother was right about you."

Ms. Brown smiled, but her eyes showed her true feelings of sadness for her daughter. She thought to herself how much work a baby is and that her daughter would really have to work that much harder. She also thought herself and how she would have another mouth to feed. She would have even less time for herself because she would have to watch the baby while Rashonda studied, did her homework, and still went after her dream. After Ms. Brown and Rashonda left, Dana saw the remaining patients.

Ms. Brown accompanied Rashonda to every doctor's visit. They signed up for Lamaze classes. Rashonda saw Peter a few times. Once he looked as if he missed her. Then it quickly faded when one of his friends approached him.

Dana and Maurice were enjoying their son. Baby Alex, as they called him, was quickly learning to maneuver his way around. Dana got a sad feeling as she thought of her little baby growing up. She invested in a camcorder and small recorder to tape all of the baby's accomplishments. She thought of Rashonda and wondered if she would actually get as much pleasure watching her baby, because she was so young herself. Maurice walked up behind Dana and kissed her neck. Dana placed her hand on his head and lovingly smiled. He turned her around and pulled her close to him. He kissed her passionately. Just then, the baby began to cry.

Maurice said, "I guess what I was thinking will have to wait. I'll get him."

"Aren't you sweet?"

"Yes. I am."

While Maurice changed and fed baby Alex, Dana finished cooking. When Maurice came downstairs, they sat and ate dinner. They enjoyed their time together. The two had been so busy at work that they didn't have time to spend together. When they arrived home, the baby took the rest of their time. After dinner they talked about their week, what had been happening at work, and then they discussed having another baby. Dana felt that they should start trying to have another baby. Maurice had his reservations because of Dana's health. She assured him that she would be fine.

Maurice took Dana's hand and said, "Well I guess we better get started."

Dana followed him up to their room.

The next day she got up. Dana got the baby ready to go to Rita's. Rita had decided to cut her work hours, so she was able to watch baby Alex. After dropping baby Alex at Rita's, Dana went to the clinic. She set things up. As the patients arrived, she noticed Rashonda with a young man. She wondered if this was the baby's father. She greeted everyone as she helped the receptionist put out new pamphlets. After they were finished, Dana went to her office.

She said to the receptionist, "You can start calling the patients." Rashonda was her third patient. When she entered her office, she brought the young man Dana saw walk in with her.

Rashonda said, "Good morning, Dr. Carrington."

"Good morning."

"This is Peter, the baby's father. He would like to hear the baby's heartbeat."

"That's great."

Dana checked Rashonda's vitals and then turned on the sonogram. She noticed Peter straining to see.

She said, "Come closer."

As he watched the baby movements on the screen, he smiled.

Peter said, "Is that really the baby?"

Dana answered, "Yes."

Just then Dana could see Peter's eyes tearing up.

He then asked, "When the baby's born, can you test its blood?"

Dana said, "Sure."

"Good."

Rashonda shifted her body. Dana could tell that she was uncomfortable with Peter's question.

Dana said, "Rashonda, I would like you to come in next week. Please make an appointment with the receptionist."

"Okay."

Dana received a call three days later from Rashonda saying that she was in labor. Dana dressed and hurried to the hospital. To Dana's surprise, when she arrived at the hospital and entered Rashonda's room, not only was Ms. Brown there but so was Peter. Dana checked Rashonda to see how close she was to delivering the baby. She was five centimeters.

Dana said, "You're five centimeters, so we are going to keep you."

She looked at Peter when she said, "We are going to take some blood."

As the contractions got closer, Dana checked Rashonda again. After she checked her, they took Rashonda into the delivery room. After forty-five minutes, Rashonda delivered a six-pound and eleven-ounce baby girl. After baby and mother were taken to their room, Dana had Peter's blood drawn. Peter held the baby.

He said, "What are you going to name her?"

Rashonda thought a few minutes and then said, "Olivia Rochai."

"What about her last name?"

"I'm going to give her my last name."

Peter looked hurt.

"I didn't want to give her your last name because you're not sure she's yours. When the results come back and you are willing to sign your name on her birth certificate, then I'll add your name."

"Fair enough."

A few days later, Peter was given the results of the paternity test. It said that he was the father of Olivia. He placed his name on the birth certificate, and Rashonda kept her word. She named the baby Olivia Rochai Brown. Peter was very attentive to the baby. He decided to stay in state to go to college. Peter wanted to stay close to the baby. He proved to be a good father. When he wasn't in school, he took Olivia to stay with him. Although he was very attentive to his baby girl, the relationship that he and Rashonda once had was no longer. They remained good friends. Rashonda was also devoted to her baby girl. When she was not in school, Rashonda spent most of the time with her. The other time she had remaining was spent going to study dance.

Chapter Four
Another Gift

Dana became pregnant. She shortened her time she spent at the clinic. When she got closer to her due date, she went on bed rest. Two months later, she delivered a healthy seven-pound, two-ounce baby girl. They named her Destiny Lora. Baby Alex was thrilled to have a baby sister. Maurice and Dana decided to get Dana's tubes tied. They both knew that each time Dana had a baby, it put more strain on her heart. She went back to work after six weeks. Dana only worked two days a week. Although she wanted to spend time with her children, she also wanted to help the women who came to the clinic. After she had returned to work three days a week, Maurice told her that the board of the hospital had decided that the clinic was losing its funding and would have to close by the end of the year.

Dana and Maurice thought it over, and with close consideration, they decided to purchase the clinic and go out on their own. They decided to name it Douglas Women's Clinic. They opened the Douglas Women's Clinic in December. On December 22 they threw a grand opening celebration and gave out gift bags filled with personal care products.

The next year was a very busy one. Trying to care for the clients and maintain the clinic was challenging. Lisa came to work for her. Lisa had gone back to school and became a midwife. Dr. Charles and Maurice took clients twice a week. They still worked at the hospital full time. Interns were also recruited to service the clinic to keep the cost down.

Dana arrived home about seven o'clock. The phone rang. She answered it.

"Hello."

"Hi, Dana. It's Rita."

"Hi, Rita. What's up?"

"I have a favor to ask."

"What is it?"

"Karen needs to intern somewhere. She has been trying to get in the hospital, but there were so many who applied she wasn't able to get in. Do you have any openings?"

"For my goddaughter of course. Tell her to come in tomorrow."

"Great, she'll be very excited."

"What is Kristie doing this summer?"

"She, unlike her sister, applied for an internship sooner and got in at Proctor and Gamble."

"That's great. I can't believe those girls are in college. Time flies."

"That's true. I don't know what to do around here sometimes."

"Why don't you come to work at the clinic? It could use as many people as possible."

"What could I do there?"

"Weren't you in school for office management at one time?"

"Yes, but I didn't finish."

"That's okay. You have some knowledge of the office, and another hand would help."

"Okay, then I'll take it."

"Great. When can you start?"

"Is next week okay?"

"Yes, that will be fine."

"Okay, I'll see you then. Talk to you later."

"Okay, bye."

Dana cooked dinner. She ate and fixed Maurice a plate because she knew that he would be home late and be hungry. She cleaned the kitchen and placed his plate in the refrigerator where he would see it. She then went upstairs. She got the children ready for bed and went to bed. The next day Karen was already at the clinic when she arrived. They greeted each other with a hug and kiss. Dana set her up at the receptionist desk. The next week she had Karen shadow her.

As the summer came to an end, Karen asked Dana if she could stay on. Dana was thrilled. Not only would she have additional help, but Karen was also an excellent worker. She was enthusiastic and well liked by the staff and clients. She also cared about people. She worked at the clinic while going to medical school. After Karen completed medical school, she was able to get into University of Medicine and Dentistry of New Jersey (UMDNJ). After she had completed her residency, Karen returned to the clinic as a medical doctor. Her parents were very proud. Kristie also became a doctor and specialized in genetics.

One day a well-dressed young woman came into the clinic. She was accompanied by a handsome soldier in his dress greens and a little girl looking to be about eleven years old. She asked to speak to Dr. Carrington. Dana came out of her office. When she came out to the waiting area, Dana immediately knew who her guests were. She walked up to the young woman and hugged her.

Dana said, "Rashonda?"

"Yes."

They hugged. Dana grabbed Rashonda's hand and motioned to the gentleman and child. She said, "Come into my office."

The three followed Dana. When they entered the office, Dana closed the door behind them. She hugged Rashonda again.

Dana said, "Who are these people?"

"Well, you know Peter."

"I thought you looked familiar. How are you?"

Peter said, "I'm fine."

Holding out her left hand, Rashonda said, "We got married five years ago. After I had Olivia, Peter went to college. We kept in touch. He came to visit the baby and kept her overnight sometimes. He then went into the air force. I sent pictures of Olivia. A couple of times on Olivia's birthday, we went out to celebrate her birthday. We started back dating seven years ago. When Peter would come home, we spent as much of his time here together as we could. Right before he left the last time before we got married, he asked me if I would be his wife. I said yes. I am dancing professionally, but I try to stay close to home. I don't like spending too much time from my family.

"I am so happy for you. Olivia is beautiful."

Rashonda and Peter said, "Thank you."

"How is your mother?"

"She's fine."

"That's good. So do you like it in Jersey?"

"No. We're visiting. Peter just got his papers for us to go to California."

"That sounds nice, and it should be great for your career."

"I do have something set up there."

"Great."

An hour later Rashonda and her family left. She promised Dana she would keep in touch. She also promised to send Dana tickets to see her in a show. They hugged. Dana was overjoyed at seeing

Rashonda. She was proud for her, of what she had overcome. Dana thought, *Who would have thought that Rashonda and Peter would end up together?* When Dana got home, she checked the mail. There was an invitation from Marsha.

It read: *You are cordially invited to the wedding of Marsha Campbell and David Dubois, Esq.*

The date: September 12

Time: 12:00 p.m.

At the First Baptist Church

10 Spring Street,

Mobile, Alabama

The second envelope included the reception invitation.

Reception immediately following at

Blacksher Hall

1056 Government Street

Mobile, Alabama

Please RSVP by August 1

Dana immediately called Marsha. No one answered the phone. The answering machine picked up. After the voice prompt, Dana said, "Hey, girl, it's Dana. Congratulations. Call me."

Several days later Marsha returned Dana's call. Dana's phone rang.

She picked it up and said, "Hello."

"Hey, girl. It's Marsha."

"Hey, yourself. Congratulations. I sent the RSVP back."

"Great. So how are things up there, your family, job, your sister, everyone?"

The two caught up on what was going on in both of their lives. After an hour on the phone, Dana said, "Well, girl, it has been wonderful talking with you, but I must go put the kids to bed."

"Okay, I'll see you soon."

After putting the children to bed, Dana cleaned up the kitchen. Maurice came home shortly after she had finished. In a joking manner, Dana said, "Oh, now you're home."

As she turned to look into Maurice's face, she saw how tired he was.

"Are you all right? You look so tired."

She walked over to him and started helping him take his clothes off.

Maurice said, "I am tired. That job is wearing me out. They have a job freeze, and all I hear is staff complaining about too much work. I understand, but there's nothing I can do."

"I know."

Dana went into the bathroom and ran a bath for the two of them. They soaked and talked for a few minutes. Maurice got quiet. She looked up and he had fallen asleep. She sat in the tub a few minutes longer and then began to wash herself and then Maurice. They ran the shower over themselves and then went to bed. The next day they were both off. They woke up, got the children bathed, dressed, and fed, and then took them to the beach. They enjoyed themselves so much that when they returned to work, they put in for a week vacation for the first week of August. They rented a house on the beach. The first morning that they were there, the couple lay around and played with the children in the water. The next two days were lazy days.

By Friday the family was relaxed and getting ready to return home. Dana awakened early Saturday. She was the first one up. She went for a walk on the beach. When she returned to the beach house, she noticed a basket on the porch. As she got closer, she became nervous because she saw it move. She cautiously moved in closer. Then she heard a gurgle. Dana no longer feared what was inside the basket but became curious. As she got closer, Dana saw a baby's head. The baby was entertaining itself with a toy. The baby smiled at her.

Dana looked around to see if she could spot anyone on the beach. Dana looked back to the baby. The baby was dressed in a pink, short, one-piece pajama and had a pink band around her head. The baby looked healthy and clean. Dana picked up the basket with the baby in it. She went into the house. She proceeded to her bedroom. When Dana entered the bedroom, Maurice had gotten up and showered. He was sitting on the side of the bed putting his socks on. Maurice looked up.

Maurice said, "What's that?"

"A baby."

"Whose is it?"

"I don't know. After I came back from walking on the beach it was on the porch."

"Did you see who left it?"

"No."

As Dana and Maurice were examining the baby, they found a note. The note said:

I watched as you were playing with your kids. They seem so happy. You see, me and Alani's father don't have much. We're too young to take care of her right now. We're both in our first year of college. I don't have any family, and David, that's Alani's father, has a mean family. They won't help. We tried. Please take care of our baby girl. We love her so much. Attached is her birth certificate. Please take her in as yours. We have signed an affidavit for you to adopt her. Don't worry, we won't bother you. We don't want our daughter to suffer. Please don't call the authorities. We don't want them involved. Raise Alani as if you had her naturally. Please don't look for us. We won't answer. It's hard enough to do this. We have to better ourselves before we can even hope to bring up a healthy adult. We ourselves have been through so much. I also put a picture of and David in the envelope, if you choose to let her know about us. Please take good care of our little angel and love her as much as you love your own.

Sincerely,

Katherine Daniels-Ban and David Ban

Dana's eyes teared up. She looked in the envelope. In it was a picture of a young couple, a pretty girl and handsome young man holding Alani. It also held the baby's birth certificate, which read that both parents were eighteen years old. They were neatly dressed in jeans. The two were kind of thin and looked like they could stand to put on a few pounds. They were all smiling. Dana thought, *Such a good-looking family. It's sad that they feel they have to go to such measures.* Dana looked at Maurice.

He said, "I'll call John."

Dana smiled and said, "Thank you."

When they arrived home, Dana checked to see if there were any messages. There weren't any. After putting their clothes away, the family ate. They decided to go shopping for some baby clothes, formula, and baby food. From the birth certificate, they could see the baby was nine months old.

The next day was Monday. Dana and Maurice only worked a half day. Maurice picked Dana up, and they went to see their attorney, John Goldman. They showed him all of the paperwork that they found with the baby. The attorney assured them that he would take care of everything for them.

At the end of August, Dana went clothes shopping to purchase clothes for the family to go to the wedding. She had purchased a plane ticket for the baby two weeks before they were to go to Alabama. The wedding was scheduled for September 10, so Dana and her family left on September 1. They wanted to spend some time with her parents. They rented a car from the airport. They took Airport Boulevard because Dana wanted to see the historic district. Dana reminisced about her younger years. She remembered catching the school bus and riding down Airport Boulevard and then turning down Spring Hill to go to school.

Just then Baby Alex, who now wanted to be called Alex, said, "Look, there's that museum we went to."

Dana asked, "You remember that?"

"Yes. I like the children's room."

"You have a good memory."

A few minutes later, they arrived at Dana mother's house. As they pulled into the driveway, Dana's mother came out of the house. As she walked toward the car, Dana and Maurice got out of the car. They met her and hugged. They returned to the car to get their bags. Her mother walked with them. Dana and Maurice opened the opposite car doors. On the driver's side, Alex jumped out and ran to his grandmother. Destiny managed to unbuckle her seat. Maurice lifted her out of her seat. When he put her down, she ran also. While this was going on, Dana was unbuckling Alani's seat belt and taking her out of her chair. Alani smiled and began to move in excitement. When Dana took her out of the car, her mother stopped, amazed. Her mouth fell opened, and with a confused look she said, "Who is this?"

Maurice said, "This is your new granddaughter, Alani."

"What? When?"

She frowned. Dana, still holding the baby, put one arm around her mother and began to tell her the story. After she had finished telling her, Mrs. Carrington asked, "Why didn't you call me?"

"I figured that I would be down here shortly and wanted to surprise you."

"I can't believe it. I feel bad for her biological parents, but I guess they did the right thing, if they thought they couldn't take care of her. I know it had to break their hearts. But she went to a good family."

Mrs. Carrington reached for Alani. Alani was hesitant.

Mrs. Carrington said to Alani, “Hey, baby. Don’t be scared. I’m your grandmom.”

She smoothed her hand over Alani’s check. Alani smiled but was still frightened.

“Okay, I won’t bother you.”

Dana said, “Is Dad awake?”

“Yes, he’s in the room. He’s not very mobile these days.”

Dana and her mother walked into the back room. Dana smiled and walked over to her father and then bent down to kiss him. Alani grabbed his face.

Dana said, “Hi, Daddy.”

He looked up. Mr. Carrington smiled and then said, “Hi, baby. Who’s this?”

“This is Alani. She is your granddaughter.”

Alani reached for him. He picked her up.

“Hi, grandbaby. How are you?”

Mr. Carrington tickled Alani, and she giggled. When she spotted Maurice, she reached for him.

Dana said, “She’s a Daddy’s girl.”

Maurice walked over to his father-in-law, shook his hand, and then took Alani from him.

Dana’s father said, “Now I know I haven’t been a hundred percent, but I don’t remember you having more than two children.”

Dana said, “I didn’t, Daddy. She’s a gift from God.”

Dana explained later at dinner. After two days, Alani acted as if she had known her new grandparents all of her life.

Dana called Marsha to let her know that she was at her mother’s. Marsha brought her children over to see Dana. They were happy to see Dana. Dana and Marsha made plans to have a couple’s night out. They went to a local night club. The DJ began to play, “For the Love that You Gave to Me” by the Delfonics.

Maurice took Dana’s hand and said, “May I have this dance?”

Dana took his hand and smiled. When they made it to the dance floor, Maurice pulled her close. Dana remembered the first time that Maurice had taken her into his arms. She still remembered the chills that she felt when he first held her. As the couple danced, it was clear to see how much they were in love. Marsha and David danced closer to Maurice and Dana.

Marsha said, "Are you sure you're not the newlyweds?"

Dana and Maurice smiled.

Maurice said, "I'll always be a newlywed."

Dana kissed him on the lips. They continued to dance. The DJ played another love song before playing fast songs. Once the fast songs were played, Dana and Maurice were reluctant to break their embrace. As they danced, Maurice said, "You still have some good moves."

"Well thank you, Mr. Douglas."

After the club closed, the couples went to a twenty-four-hour diner. At the diner, Marsha broke the news to Dana that she was pregnant.

Dana asked, "Do the children know?"

Marsha answered, "No. I plan to tell them sometime after the wedding."

"Wow. I can't believe you're starting all over."

"I know."

Dana reached over and hugged her.

"I wish you all the happiness."

"Thank you."

As it got lighter outside, Maurice said, "I think we better get back."

The couples said their good-byes. Dana and Maurice headed back to Dana's mother's house. It was five o'clock. Just as they were entering the house, they heard Alani crying. They went into the room to get her. After Dana picked Alani up, her mother entered the room.

She said, "You just getting in?"

Dana answered, "Yes."

"Did you have a nice time?"

"Yes, Mom. It was nice. We haven't been out in a long time, and it was nice being with another couple."

"Good. Give me the baby. I'll feed her. Get some rest."

"Are you sure?"

"Yes. Now go."

Dana kissed her mother and then took Maurice by the hand and led him into their room. They showered together and then went to bed. When they awakened, Dana and Maurice found the house to be empty. The couple looked outside. Dana's mother and father were sitting outside watching the children play on the swing set. Alani was sitting in Dana father's lap enjoying watching her siblings play. Dana and Maurice went outside. Her mother offered them some lemonade. They poured themselves a glass and sat down. Alex and Destiny waved at their parents. Dana and Maurice kneeled over and kissed Alani. She giggled and then returned her attention back to her siblings. Alani giggled off and on as she watched her siblings play. A few times the children would run up to her and play with Alani.

Later that day, Marsha and David came over. They too sat in the backyard with the Dana and her family. Mary and her family came over as well. Mrs. Carrington decided to cook on the grill. Marsha's children came over later. At about eight, Dana's father turned in. He told everyone how much he enjoyed their company. The smaller children were put to bed by nine. The teens and adults stayed up, playing music, playing cards, and talking about old times until two in the morning. By three, they all began to go home. Before Marsha and David left, the couple decided that Marsha and Dana would spend the day together. David and Maurice took that time to go to a ball game, for the following day Marsha and David were getting married. While Marsha and Dana enjoyed being pampered, David and Maurice enjoyed watching a baseball game. When night came, Dana and Marsha went to her bridal shower, which was being thrown by her friend Tina. The group played games and snacked on hors d'oeuvres. During this time David and Maurice went to the Hilton Hotel, where a bachelor party was being thrown for David.

Back at Tina's house, she was opening gifts. The doorbell rang. Marsha wondered who could be coming now since it was getting late and everyone she could think of was already there. Ten minutes later, two six-feet men, one cocoa brown and the other bronze, stepped into the door. They were well built but not overly muscular. One was dressed in an army uniform and the other air force. Music started playing, and the two men began dancing. She then realized that they were strippers. The guy in the army uniform asked, "Where's the bride to be?"

Everyone pointed to Marsha. She was taken to a chair that had been placed in the middle of the living room floor. The two stripers began dancing in front of her. Some of the women cheered. Marsha tried to look away, but the men were on both sides of her. She blushed as they took articles of clothes off. Both men realized that it was a bit much for her and they were making her feel uncomfortable, so they moved on to the more rowdy women in the room. Marsha breathed a sigh of relief. She laughed along with the others as her sister Carry, who was always so prim and proper, grabbed hold of one of the strippers and began dancing with him in a very provocative way. After they had stripped down to their G-strings, the music was turned off. They wrapped themselves in towels. The women clapped. The men thanked Marsha for being a good sport. Tina escorted them out and paid them.

David and Maurice were enjoying watching sports with David's friends at his bachelor party. During the game, drinks were being served. At ten there was a knock on the door. David's friend Milton answered the door. Three women dressed in trench coats and stilettos walked in. Milton grabbed David by the arm, and another friend grabbed a chair. Milton walked David to the chair. David sat in it. Music was turned on, and the women began to perform. One of the women tried to give David a lap dance, but he gently moved her off of him. Milton yelled, "I'll take one."

The woman danced over to him. The other women were dancing and entertaining the other men.

Milton asked, "What's your name, baby?"

She responded, "Candy."

"Are you as sweet as your name?"

"Yes I am."

Milton licked her back.

"Ooh, you are sweet. Do you taste like this all over?"

"Yes I do."

"Can I taste you?"

"That will cost you more."

"How much?"

"$200.00."

"Let's go."

He tapped her on her behind. She got off of his lap. They headed to the back bedroom. Maurice tapped David to look at Milton.

"Man, look at your boy."

"Man, he's grown."

After some time, Milton emerged from the back bedroom. Candy followed close behind him, holding his hand. The other women had stopped dancing and were mingling with the other men. David and Maurice were watching the sports channel. By dawn everyone had crashed out. The men were awaked by the women packing up their items they had brought to the party. As Candy was leaving, Milton handed her his card. She smiled and put it in her bra. She lightly kissed him on the lips. After the women had gone, one of the men said, "Man, you must have put it on her."

Milton said, "You know it."

The men began to leave. David thanked all of them for coming. David and Maurice left. David remained behind. As they were leaving the hotel, they noticed Candy returning to the hotel. The three smiled but didn't speak. Once they were in David's car, Maurice said, "I guess he did put it down and she's going back for seconds."

"Man, Milton is known for pulling women; I just hope he will show up at the wedding. He is the best man."

"Hopefully he'll be able to walk."

They both laughed.

David dropped Maurice at his in-laws' home. Maurice rang the doorbell. Dana opened the door. He lightly kissed her lips.

She said, "Did you miss me?"

"Whenever we're apart."

"Did you have a good time?"

"It was entertaining. How about you?"

"Same here."

They showered together and then lay down. After two hours, they reluctantly got up to get ready for the wedding. They arrived at the church and were seated by the ushers.

Dana said, "This is beautiful."

On the end of each pew there were maroon, pink, and white roses, with miniature calla lilies with white organza with beaded trim hanging down. There were flowers all through the church. As the wedding party began to come in, the music started playing. A singer sang, "Always and Forever." As the flower girls marched toward the altar, they dropped pink, maroon, and white petals. After the maid of honor made her way to the altar, the guests were motioned to stand. Two ushers began to roll out the aisle runner. Marsha was escorted in by her son. When they reached the altar, Marsha's son took her arm from around his and placed her hand in David's. He then sat down. Maurice was pleased to see Milton had made it to the wedding. When the minister asked, "Who gives this woman?" Marsha's son stood up and said, "I do."

Marsha and David recited their vows. The minister pronounced them husband and wife. David kissed Marsha. Everyone stood up and clapped. The guests followed the couple as they exited the church and got into their waiting limo. After the couple had arrived at the reception, the wedding party was introduced. Marsha and David danced together for the first time as husband and wife. After David and Marsha danced, the wedding party joined them. When the dance was over, dinner was served. After dinner, dance music was played. David and Marsha began to mingle. Maurice looked out onto the dance floor, to his surprise, he saw Milton dancing with a woman who looked familiar. He asked Dana to dance. Maurice and Dana danced a while and then he remembered. Maurice couldn't believe that Milton was so taken with the stripper that he would invite her to someone's wedding, nor could he believe that she was so taken with him that she would come. He thought, *I guess there's someone for everyone.*

As the bride and groom walked around the room thanking everyone for coming, David stopped to talk with Milton.

David said, "Hey, man, I was kind of worried about you showing up."

Milton responded, "I don't believe you. You are my best friend, and this is an important day for you. I couldn't let you down. We had fun last night, right?"

Milton smiled and hit David on the arm.

Looking at Milton's guest, David said, "I see you're still enjoying yourself."

"Oh, excuse my manners. David, this is Tiffany Banks. She is a nursing student."

David reached out his hand. He said, "Oh, nice to formally meet you."

Tiffany extended her hand with a smile and said, "Same here. Congratulations. It was a beautiful ceremony."

"Thank you."

David excused himself and returned to the side of his bride. After the reception was over, Dana hugged David and Marsha. They said their good-byes. The next day, Dana packed up the family's belongings. They said their good-byes to her parents and then headed to the airport. Once they boarded the airplane, everyone quickly fell asleep. When the plane touched down in Newark, everyone exited the plane. When they arrived home. Dana checked the messages. Their attorney had called. She played the message.

"Hi, Dana, I know you guys aren't back yet, but give me a call when you get in."

The next day Dana called the attorney. She was told that they had a court date on Monday, September 25. Dana purchased two pink dresses, one for Destiny and the other for Alani. She purchased a suit for Alex as well. When the big day came, everyone was dressed as if to have their portrait taken. Dana was very nervous. Maurice noticed and held her hand. They were waiting outside of the courtroom thirty minutes before being called.

The sheriff's officer called, "Douglas."

Dana answered, "Here"

He escorted them into the courtroom. To their surprise, they were seated at a table. When the judge was made aware they were ready, she entered the courtroom and sat at the table with them.

The judge said, "Good morning, I'm Judge Classe." The judge looked at all three children. She said, "All of your children are beautiful."

The judge went through the procedure. After the paperwork

was completed and orders were signed, the family took pictures. The family was escorted out of the courtroom. They went out to lunch.

When the group arrived home, Alex said, "Alani is my real sister now."

Maurice answered, "Yes, and you have to take care of her like you do Destiny."

"I will."

Alex kissed Alani on the cheek. She giggled and grabbed his face.

A month later, Dana's phone rang. She picked it up. Dana said, "Hello."

"Hi, girl."

"Marsha?"

"Yes. What, you've already forgotten me?"

"Of course not. How's married life?"

"It's wonderful."

"I'm glad things are going well. How are the children?"

"They are fine."

"Guest what?"

"What?"

"Girl you know the guy who was the best man, Milton?"

"Yes."

"Well he's getting married next week to a stripper who was at David bachelor's party."

"Really? I guess she was good."

"You know he brought her to my wedding?"

"What? That girl who was with him is a stripper? She was dressed so nice and they seemed like they had been together longer than one night."

"I know he wasn't dating anyone prior to our wedding, but I thought maybe they had known each other longer than one night.

I can't believe he's sprung like that. He is known for being a Casanova."

"I guess the saying is true, there's someone for everyone. I hope things work out for them, being that he's a Casanova."

"David told me that she is finishing nursing school."

"Wow. Well at least he doesn't have to worry about her finding another job."

"I just can't believe someone snagged him and it had to take a stripper to do it. You won't believe this either. Do you remember my shower? Do you know my prim and proper sister Carry? Well, she slept with that stripper she was all over."

"What? Are you serious? I know she was all over him, but I would have never thought she would sleep with him. How did you find out?"

"My other sister told me that she called Carry on her cell phone. She was surprised at a man answering her phone. She drilled him. He gave his stage name, and she remembered."

"All I can say is wow."

"That's enough about down here. What's going on with you?"

"We adopted Alani."

"Really? That is some good news. It is crazy about her parents giving her to you. But they couldn't have given her to a better family."

"Thank you. We're happy. She is a smart baby. I wish the parents well. So how are you doing?"

"We're doing great. I am so in love with David. I never imagined loving someone the way that I love him. He is a good guy, caring, and tries to do everything to make me happy and comfortable. I am doing great. The children are very helpful."

"That's good. Have you told them that you're pregnant?"

"Yes. They are excited and looking forward to the baby being born."

"That's good. I'm glad that everything has worked out for you."

"I know you'll say that you had nothing to do with it, but I still believe that you are a blessing."

"Thank you."

"Oh, I almost forgot to tell you the punch line about Carry sleeping with the stripper."

"What is it?"

"She's pregnant."

"Really? I am shocked."

"Yeah, so were the rest of us."

"So what is she going to do?"

"She's keeping the baby. She's too old to have an abortion, because she may not get another chance. Do you know this was her first time? She said that she was saving herself."

"How old is she?"

"She's thirty-nine."

"Oh. Does the guy know?"

"No. It was a one-night stand."

"Wow."

"Well, I better let you go."

"Okay, I'll talk to you soon."

As months passed, the clinic was doing well. There were so many cuts at the hospital that Maurice decided to work full time at the clinic. Dana enjoyed spending more time with her husband. They had lunch together every day and made decisions together about the clinic. Marsha had a baby boy. She and David were very excited. David didn't have any children prior to being with Marsha. He was very close to her children, but having a son that was biological brought great pleasure. The children were happy to have a new baby brother. The two older children were living on their own but came by frequently to visit with their little brother. Marsha and David decided that she would stay home. David was doing well at the firm, so he could afford Marsha staying home. She enjoyed it because she didn't get the chance to stay home with her other children and always felt guilty leaving them.

Then years later, Dana received a letter at the clinic. It didn't have a return address. She wondered who it was from. She curiously opened it. It began:

Dear Dr. Douglas,

I want to first start out by saying thank you for being an exceptional person. My husband and I have become successful people with few worries because of your caring and generosity. Ten years ago, we were in a desperate state. That day seeing you and your family gave us hope. I guess you're wondering who I am. My husband and I made the most heartbreaking decision we think anyone could make. We had many sleepless nights, but after watching your family, we knew we wanted this for our daughter. It was the hardest thing we have ever had to do. I want you to know that I am a surgeon and my husband is CEO at a successful company. We made sure that we didn't get ourselves in a bind again and stayed focused on our dreams. If you ever decide that you want or need to tell Alani that she was a gift, just tell her to put an ad in the paper saying looking for the people at the beach. I'll know it's from her. If you decided never to tell her, that's fine too. I just ask that you put in the paper who she becomes. Thank you again, and we are forever grateful.

Katherine and David

A tear came into Dana's eyes. That night she showed Maurice the letter. He asked Dana what she wanted to do with the information. They both decided to keep the adoption to themselves and to post an ad in the paper when Alani grew up and list her accomplishments.

A few months later, Dana and Maurice were watching the news. After the weather report, the reporter announced, "This just in: a woman has fatally shot and killed her live-in boyfriend. Further details to come." As the police were bringing the woman out of her New York high-rise apartment, Dana sat up. She couldn't believe what she was seeing.

She said, "Maurice, do you know who that is?"

Maurice looked closer and thought, but he couldn't think who it was.

He said, "No. Who is it?"

"That's Sandy."

"Sandy?"

"Yes. Remember when we were going to get married and this nurse at the hospital said she was pregnant by you?"

"Oh. Okay, I remember. I wonder who the unfortunate guy was."

"Me too. I sometimes wondered what happened to her."

Just then the phone rang. Dana picked it up.

"Hello?"

"Hi, Dana, it's Lisa."

"Lisa. Hi, Lisa. How are you?"

"I'm fine."

"What's up?"

"Did you see the news?"

"Yes, about Sandy?"

"Yes."

"Do you know who the boyfriend was?"

"No. They didn't say."

"It was Dave."

"Your old boyfriend?"

"Yes. I guess he hit the wrong woman."

"I can't believe those two crazies got together."

"I had heard something a while back. I was happy that he finally moved on. I thought he had gotten help for his anger problem. I guess it didn't help."

"I guess not. I can't believe those two got together, and I really don't believe she killed him."

"Life is funny that way."

"So what's been going on in your life?"

"Well, I've been keeping busy. Nothing spectacular. I heard about the success with the clinic and your new baby."

"Yeah, things are great. Hey, I'm having a dinner party in two weeks. Would you like to come?"

"Are you sure?"

"Of course. There will be a lot of people you know."

"Okay, I'll be there. What time?"

"Six-thirty."

"Okay, I'll see you then."

When Dana got off the phone, she filled Maurice in.

He said, "It's a small world. Who would think those two would meet and form a relationship?"

"I know."

With that, they went up, tucked their children in bed, and gave them an extra kiss good night.

The next two weeks were busier than usual. Dana was preparing for their dinner party. The night of the party Dana put on a form-fitting knee-length navy blue dress. She liked this dress because it met each curve perfectly. She accented the dress with a diamond necklace, matching earrings, and bracelet. When Maurice saw Dana, he stopped to admire her. Dana smiled as she saw the passion in his eyes. He came over and put his arms around her waist. Maurice started kissing her with small pecks. He then pulled her closer and kissed her with more intensity. While kissing Dana, he placed his hand on her behind. Dana couldn't resist his touch. An hour later, she redressed and went downstairs to make sure everything was set up the way she wanted. As the guests arrived, Dana and Maurice greeted them together. Once everyone had arrived, Dana and Maurice split up and mingled with their guests. Dana made her way to Lisa. They talked for a while, getting caught up with each other's lives. Lisa asked to see the children. Dana took her upstairs. It was still fairly early, so the children were still awake.

After they came back downstairs, Lisa said, "Your children are beautiful. Alex looks just like his father, and he's all grown up."

"Yes, he has. He's just finished New Jersey Institute of Technology. He is going to be an architect."

"Wow. I'm so happy for you. Can you believe so much has happened since we first met?"

"I know."

Just then Dr. Charles walked over. His good looks had not changed. He was six feet tall, about 180 pounds, all muscles, and well dressed. He was forty-five, but looked like he was in his thirties. He kissed and hugged both Dana and Lisa.

He said, "Hey, ladies, would one of you like to accompany me on the dance floor?"

Maurice, standing behind him, said, "This one is mine." He took Dana's hand and led her onto the dance floor.

Dr. Charles said to Lisa, "Would you like to dance?"

Lisa said, "Sure."

Dr. Charles led Lisa onto the dance floor. They danced for a while, and then a slow song was played. When Lisa began to walk away, Dr. Charles took hold of her hand, and with a smooth twist of his wrist, Lisa was in his arms. They swayed to the music. After the song was over, Maurice and Dana walked over to them and whispered, "The song stopped."

Lisa looked up. She turned red when she realized that Dr. Charles was holding her as if they were a couple. He looked at her and said, "Don't mind them; they're just jealous because we dance better than them."

They all laughed. The party went on until 2:00 a.m. When the party was over and everyone had said their good-byes, Dr. Charles asked Lisa for her number. She hesitantly gave him her cell phone number. A week later, Dr. Charles called Lisa's cell phone. The voicemail picked up. Dr. Charles left a message.

"Hi, Lisa, this is Michael, Dr. Charles. I was just checking to see how things were going with you. When you get a chance, give me a call. I can be reached at (945) 333-952. Hope to talk to you soon. Bye."

Later that evening after Lisa was relaxing, she checked her cell phone for missed calls. There was only one. It was from Dr. Charles. She listened to the message. She thought how nice his voice sounded on the phone. She looked at the clock. It was 8:00 p.m. She thought to herself, *I wonder if it's too late to call him.* Lisa decided to make the call. Michael answered on the second ring.

"Hello."

"Hi, it's Lisa."

"Hi, Lisa. How are you?"

"I'm fine. How about yourself?"

"I'm great. I wondered if you would return my call."

"Why?"

"Sometimes women don't like to call men."

"I don't mind as long as I'm not the only one calling."

"I'm glad. Listen, before I forget, I have tickets to the Performing Art Center in Newark, next Friday to see a comedy review. Would you like to come?"

"What time is the show?"

"Seven. Is that okay?"

"That's fine. I'm actually off next Friday."

"That's great. Then you'll be rested."

"What else do you have planned?"

"Nothing, but some women like to leave right after because

they've worked all day or end up being late because they were trying to rest."

"Dr. Charles."

"Michael, please."

"Michael, I think that you've had some bad dates, but please don't judge all women by your past bad experiences. Let me just tell you this. I was in an abusive relationship a long time ago. I believe you are aware of one of your past accountancies being aired on the five o'clock news a few weeks ago, Sandy."

"Yes. You knew her?"

"Yes, and I would like to share that the guy she killed was the guy I dated, and he is the guy that abused me. I would also like to add that I have not dated since."

"I didn't know that. How long has it been?"

"Eleven years."

"Really?"

"Yes."

"Is there any reason why?"

"I thought I needed some time off, and when I was ready, no one came along."

"I can't believe no man has approached you."

"Some have come, but for one reason or another, I decided not to go out with them."

"I hope you don't stand me up."

"There's one thing about me: if I tell you I'm going to do something, I do it. With the other guys I never gave them my number, nor did I take theirs."

"So I should feel privileged?"

"Yes you should."

They continued talking until eleven o'clock.

Michael said, "Well, I think that I should let you go. I will be away a few days on a business trip. Can I call you when I get back?"

"Sure. I'll talk to you then."

"Sleep well."

"You too."

They hung up. Lisa got ready for bed. As she lay in her bed, Lisa thought how refreshing it was to have a man to talk to for a change. She soon drifted off to sleep. Before Michael went to bed, he made sure he packed his suitcase for his trip. When he got into bed, he reached over to set the alarm clock. He lay back thinking about his conversation with Lisa. He chuckled to himself and said, "This might be the one." He then drifted off to sleep.

The trip lasted longer than Michael expected. He arrived back in Newark on Monday. After checking his voicemail and making some important phone calls, Michael took a chance and called Lisa.

She answered, "Hello."

"Hi Lisa?"

"Yes."

"This is Michael. I hope I'm not disturbing you."

"Hi, Michael. No you're not." She didn't want to seem excited. She went on to say, "How was your trip?"

"It was productive. I'm happy to be back."

"What, you missed me?"

"Yes I did."

"Yeah, sure."

"I did. It was nice talking to you before I left. It's refreshing to talk to you."

"I'm flattered."

"So are you ready for Friday?"

"Yes." She didn't want to seem too excited.

"I look forward to seeing you again."

Lisa smiled. Michael went on, "So what do you look for in a man?"

"I look for someone who can support me not just financially but emotionally. Don't get me wrong, I can take care of myself, but it would be nice if I could rely on someone other than myself."

"What do you expect from a relationship?"

"It's not that I expect, but if it's a good relationship I would look to one day make things permanent."

She didn't want to say marriage because she didn't want to frighten him away. She went on, "So what are you looking for in woman, and are you looking for a committed relationship?"

"I look for a woman who is attractive to me. What I mean by that is I like a woman who is confident and sure of herself. She has pride and carries herself as if sure of herself. She's beautiful inside and out. She is willing to stick with her man through thick and thin. I don't want a gold digger. I do plan to get married one day, so I want a woman who is spiritual and hasn't been around the block too much. I understand if you have been in a relationship for a long time that you've had sex probably a lot, but I don't want a woman who had so many partners she can't count them. No, I don't ask for the number, nor do I want to know, but a man kind of knows if you're free with it."

"Wow. You really have high expectations."

"If I don't, I can't expect you to have it about me. When I am with a lady, I want to hold her with pride. I don't want to be embarrassed by her past. On a lighter note, how do you want to do this? Do you want me to pick you up at your place, or do you want to meet at the PAC?"

"You know, I hadn't thought about it, but I think it will be all right if you come to my house to pick me up."

"Okay great. What is your address?"

"It's 333 Highland Avenue in Orange."

"Okay. Is six o'clock okay to pick you up? I would like to get to the PAC early enough to get a good parking space and have time for us to talk before the show."

"That's fine."

"Well I think that I've kept you long enough. I want you to get your beauty rest. Not that you need it."

"Okay, then I'll see you Friday at six o'clock."

"Good night."

Lisa laid back in bed thinking about their conversation. She thought, *I like this guy.* After placing the phone down Michael couldn't believe how taken he was with Lisa. The next few days were busy for the two. Lisa reached out to Dana. Dana had worked until seven o'clock. When she arrived home, the phone was ringing. She dropped her things on the table in the foyer.

She picked up the receive. "Hello."

"Hi, Dana. It's Lisa. Did I catch you at a bad time?"

"No. I was just getting in. Why, what's up?"

"Do you want me to call you back?"

"No. It's okay, we can talk. What's going on?"

"I just called to talk and ask your opinion about something."

"Okay."

Dana sat down at the desk in the foyer and began looking through the mail that she had just placed there.

Lisa began, "Well, Dr. Charles and I have been talking on the phone."

Dana put the mail down to listen more attentively. Dana said, "Really? I knew you guys hit it off."

"Yes. He asked me to go out to a comedy show at the PAC on Friday."

"What? That's great."

"So I take it that he's a nice guy."

"Yes. You didn't know him when you worked at the hospital?"

"Not really. You know I was dating Dave and you know what was going on with me then."

"Yes, I know."

"He seems like a nice guy. I know this sounds crazy, but even though I haven't gone out with him and I've only talked to him a few times, I like him. You know at your party he was so charming."

"You know he helps out at the clinic and does it for free. I haven't heard anything bad about him. Girl, just go and have some fun."

"Doesn't this sound familiar?"

"Yeah. You're right. You gave me the same advice many years ago."

"Well, I'm going to let you go."

"Okay. Call me next week. Let me know how your date goes."

"Will do. Thanks for your ear."

"Anytime."

When Friday came, Lisa got up early to go shopping for an outfit to wear on her date. She didn't have anything she thought was nice enough to go out on a date. She went to a few stores before deciding on a two-piece burgundy long-sleeved pants set. Lisa tried it on and liked the way it fit the curves of her body. She accented it with a cream camisole underneath the jacket, which she decided she would keep close. Lisa also brought a pair of medium-length gold earrings, a necklace, and a bracelet to match. She thought to herself, *I definitely have to go shopping more and I need to get some dressier clothes.* After paying for the clothes, she went shopping for shoes. She picked a pair of three-inch beige open-toe shoes with a matching purse. She also decided to go to Victoria's Secret to purchase lingerie. Even though she had no plans of anyone seeing them, she thought it would make her feel sexy. After leaving the mall, Lisa stopped at a McDonald's that was on her way home. Lisa didn't want to be too hungry when she went out. She arrived back home at twelve o'clock. She decided to take a nap. It was two-thirty when she awakened. Lisa steamed her clothes to get the few wrinkles out. She showered and then began getting dressed.

By six she was ready. Michael was on time. He rang her doorbell. She gathered her purse and headed for the door. She didn't want to offend him, so Lisa made sure there was no reason for him to have to come in.

When Lisa opened the door she said, "Hi."

Michael leaned over and gave her a friendly kiss on her cheek. She smiled. He asked, "Are you ready?"

"Yes."

She was pleased that he did not try to gain access into her home. Michael took her hand and escorted her to his car. He opened the door and helped her in.

Michael said, "You look beautiful."

"Thank you. You look good yourself."

Michael wore a dark blue suit with a striped shirt. As Michael drove to the art center, they made light conversation, talking about their week. Thirty minutes later, they arrived at the PAC. Michael parked the car. He exited the car and then walked around to the passenger's side of the car and opened the car door. He put his hand out to Lisa. She took his hand, and he helped her out of the car. They walked into the center. The two were in the third row from the front of the stage. Lisa was impressed.

Michael said, "You know I'm going to have a hard time paying attention to the show."

"Why?"

"Lady, you look good. I'm kind of happy that the lights are dim."

"You are too much."

"No, you are. I'm glad though."

When the show began, the theater quieted. Michael asked if Lisa minded him putting his arm around her chair. She permitted him to.

On occasion as they laughed at the jokes, they glanced at each other. One of the comedians said, "Hey, you."

Michael responded, "Me," pointing at himself.

The comedian said, "Yeah. What are you newlyweds? Look at you all lovey dovey. You can tell the new ones."

"No, our first date."

"Oh, I see. You trying to get in there. She's ready, man."

The audience laughed. Lisa turned red and put her head down. "Aah, look at her, she's blushing. Man, your mac must be on. Okay, I'll leave you two love birds alone. Come back in five years. We'll see if she has that glow then."

The audience laughed again. Michael caressed Lisa's shoulder in a comforting effort. After the show, they decided to go to the after party. They mingled with some of the other guests. The couple danced to a few songs. At two o'clock, Michael asked Lisa if she was ready to go home. She said yes, but she really didn't want the night to end. On the drive home, Michael made light conversation. When they arrived at her home, Michael escorted her to the door and lightly kissed her cheek. Lisa was happy for this because she didn't know how she would have reacted if he kissed her on the lips. Lisa was very taken with Michael, and it didn't help that she hadn't been with a man in so many years. But she didn't want to rush into anything. He waited until she entered her home. He waved at her and then went to his car. He drove home. Michael took off his clothes and then went to take a shower. As he washed himself, he thought of Lisa. He couldn't believe that he was getting aroused. He rinsed off and got out of the shower. Michael dried off. He thought to himself, *Man, what is going on? You have only talked to this woman a few times and went out once.* He got into bed and fell asleep. The next day Michael awakened at nine-thirty in the morning. He knew Lisa had the day off, so he took a chance and called her. She answered the phone.

"Hello."

"Hi, Lisa, I hope I didn't wake you."

"No. I've been up awhile."

What he didn't know was that she had awakened early thinking about him.

"I know you said that you were off today. By chance, do you have any plans today?"

"No, not really."

"Would you like to spend the day with me?"

She said with a calm voice, "Sure." But inside her heart was leaping.

"Can you be ready by twelve?"

"Yes. Where are we going?"

"I thought maybe we can go down the shore."

"That sounds nice. I haven't been down the shore in a long time."

"Great, then I'll see you at twelve."

"Okay. Bye."

Lisa looked in her closet. Lisa had casual clothes but not what she would have liked to wear on her second date with Michael. She finally decided on a navy blue skort. She matched it with a short-sleeve button-down blouse and navy blue two-inch sandals. Lisa didn't want to dress too casually because she wanted to be prepared if they ended up in a nice restaurant for dinner. Lisa also put on the jacket that went to the skort. When Michael arrived, she was ready. He rang her doorbell, and again she had everything she needed. She answered the door.

Michael said, "Hi." He kissed her on the cheek and asked, "Are you ready?"

She smiled and answered, "Yes."

Lisa locked her door. Michael escorted her to his car and opened the door for her. She thought how refreshing it was to have a gentleman around. After helping Lisa into the car, Michael walked around to the driver's side of the car. As he walked to get into the car, she watched and admired how good-looking he was. This was really the first time she had seen him in the day time. He stood six feet. She noticed that he had on a dress shirt. Because it was fitted, she could see his muscles in his chest and a washboard six-pack stomach. When he got into the car, she looked away. Michael smiled because he knew that she was checking him out. He got into the car and put on his seat belt. After pulling out, he said, "You look beautiful."

"Thank you. You look nice yourself."

"So did you have a nice time last night?"

"Yes. How about you?"

"I was with you. Of course I had a good time. Did you sleep well last night?"

"Yes."

"I fell asleep thinking of you."

Lisa couldn't believe he was telling her this. She responded, "Oh, yeah?"

"You think I'm running a line, but I'm serious. I really like you. That's why I called you this morning. I want to get to know you."

"That's nice to hear. I have to admit I was pleased to hear your voice on the other end of my phone."

"Okay. I'm making progress."

"So what do you have planned for us today?"

"Do you like the beach?"

"I love the beach."

"How about the water?"

"It's nice."

"Have you eaten?"

"I had breakfast."

"Okay. Well when we get to the shore area, we'll stop to get something to eat and then go shopping for suits. Is that okay?"

"That's fine."

They continued talking throughout the ride. When they arrived at Seaside Heights, they went to eat at a seafood restaurant.

Michael asked, "Forgive me, I didn't ask if you like or can eat seafood."

Lisa smiled. "I forgive you. Yes, I love most seafood."

"Good."

They entered the Seaside Crab House Seafood Emporium. Once they were seated and given their menus, the waiter left to get their drink orders. They both ordered virgin drinks. When the waiter returned, they ordered the oysters, stuffed crab with shrimp, lobster tails, and sushi. When their food was brought to them, they thanked the waiter and then began to eat. A few times as they tried the different foods, Michael fed Lisa. After they finished eating, Michael paid the bill and they exited the restaurant. They walked to the clothing shops. They both picked out bathing suits and beach towels. When the two went up to the register, Michael put all of the items together. Lisa moved her items in an attempt to separate them.

The cashier asked, "Are these on the same bill?"

Michael said, "Yes," simultaneously with Lisa's "No."

The cashier looked at both of them. Michael said, "It's my treat. You didn't plan on shopping."

Lisa argued, "No, it's okay."

Michael insisted, "Don't worry about it."

Lisa said, "Are you sure?"

Michael smiled at her uneasy look.

He said, "It's all right. This is my pleasure. You don't owe me anything."

After the cashier rang up the items and handed Michael's credit card back to him, she winked at Lisa and in a whispered tone said for only Lisa to hear, "He's a keeper."

Lisa looked uneasy. They left the shop and headed for the beach. They went into the shower/changing facilities and changed into their bathing suits. When Lisa came out of the changing facility, Michael was waiting outside of it. She could tell from the way he looked at her, she looked good. He smiled and held his hand out. Lisa took hold of it. As they walked onto the beach, they held hands. Michael let go of her hand when he went to pay for the beach umbrella. They went to the first open area where there weren't too many people. Michael put the umbrella up. They laid the beach towels down.

Michael said, "Lisa, you are a very attractive woman."

"Why, thank you."

"Do you work out?'

"Not as much as I would like, but I try to get at least three times a week."

"Well it shows. Would you like to go in the water?"

"Sure."

They splashed around in the water for a while. Michael tried to grab her. She ran. He caught her and picked her up. She tried to push him away. He held on to her. She stopped fighting. They laughed. In just an instant, they stopped laughing. They looked into each other's eyes. Michael, still holding her, kissed her on the lips. She returned his kiss. Michael continued to hold her in his arms as they kissed. She wrapped her arms around his neck one at a time. They kissed until a ball hit Michael in the back. He abruptly stopped kissing her. A young man ran up to him laughing, saying, "I'm sorry, man."

Michael said, "No problem."

Michael looked at Lisa. She smiled and said, "Can I get down now?"

Michael smiled and then put her down. They walked back to where they had set up their umbrella. Michael smoothed his hand over Lisa's face and kissed her again. She smoothed one hand down the back of his head and rested it on his neck. After a few minutes of kissing, a child about five walked over to them and said, "My mommy and daddy do that."

The child looked back at his mother, pointing at Michael and Lisa. He said, "Look, Mommy, he loves her."

The child's mother yelled to him, "You come back over here and leave those people alone."

The child said, "Bye."

Michael smiled and said, "Bye." Michael turned to Lisa and said, "I guess I better wait for a better time."

Lisa answered, "Yes I think so."

Michael asked, "So are you enjoying yourself?"

"Yes. It's nice here."

"Yes, the view is very nice."

Lisa looked at him and saw that he was looking at her with desire in his eyes.

She said, "I was talking about the scenery."

"So was I." Michael laughed. "So what do you do with your spare time?"

"I read, go to church, and occasionally if a movie comes out that looks good, I go see it."

"Who do you go with?"

"Myself. After dealing with people all day, it's nice to have quiet."

"Do you have any friends?"

"Yes, but I don't talk to them often, because they have their own lives. I don't want to be the third wheel and I get tired of people trying to fix me up."

"I'm having a hard time believing that you haven't dated in over ten years."

"Believe it. I sometimes think about it, but I don't want to have sex to get a date. Guys seem to think that you have to have sex after they take you out. I'm not prudish but I'm not desperate and I'm not a test model. Enough of me. What about you? When was the last time you were in a relationship?"

"It's been a while. It was very short. Things just didn't mesh. I've gone out on dates here and there, but that's all it was."

"Have you ever been married? Have any children?"

"I've never been married. I was in a committed relationship once, but things didn't work out. There was a woman who said she was pregnant once. I discovered that she wasn't wrapped too tight, and we took care of it."

"Do you want to have children?"

"I would like to have children when I get married."

"So you don't have a problem with commitment?"

"No. I'm tired of the games some women play, and I would like to come home one day to the same beautiful woman."

He lightly kissed her on her lips.

"Let's go. Are you hungry?"

"Not too much."

He stood up and said, "Well let's get out of these clothes."

He held his hand out to Lisa. She took it. He helped her up. They walked to the beach showers and changing facilities. Once they changed, they got into Michael's car and drove off. A half hour later they arrived at the Luna Rosa Restaurant. They parked and went in. As the two were seated, the waiter asked if they wanted a drink. Michael asked Lisa, "Do you drink alcoholic beverages?"

"Not too often. What did you have in mind?"

"They have the best wine I've ever tasted. They make it themselves. Would you like to try it?"

"I don't like it dry."

"That's fine, they have several different kinds."

The waiter said, "Very good. I will bring you a bottle."

Lisa asked, "So how do you know about this place? Did you bring any of your dates here?"

"No. I actually stumbled upon this place after a breakup."

"If it's not too much to ask, can I ask what happened?"

The waiter returned with the wine. He poured it for them and took their order. Once he left, Michael began, "It's been a long time, but I had been dating this woman for two years. I thought that we had a good relationship. I figured I'd ask her to marry me and we'd go together to purchase the engagement ring. I brought her down the shore for a weekend getaway. She seemed happy to be going. When we got to the hotel it was late, because we left after I got off work. Although it was late, she still seemed happy. After we checked in, I asked if she was hungry. She said yes, so we ordered in. While we were eating, a look came her face. I had a gut feeling that something had gone bad. She looked at me with sadness in her eyes and said, 'I can't do this. I've tried to live by your schedule, but I can't.' With that I knew nothing I said could change the way she felt. We stayed the night. She had a close cousin who lived in Cape May. I drove her there. As I was driving back north, I saw this restaurant. I hadn't eaten, and I figured I'd in a morbid way celebrate being single again. I wasn't too broken up because even though I really liked her, I wasn't in love."

The waiter came back with their food. He asked them if he could get them anything else. Both of them answered no.

Lisa asked, "Have you ever been in love?"

Michael answered, "Not really. I have liked two women very much, but it never went any further. With going to college and then to med school and trying to find a job, I wasn't interested in getting serious about anyone. The first woman was during my college years and the second woman I told you about. Have you ever been in love, been married, or had any children?"

"I've been in love once. It was the last relationship that I was in. He was physically abusive. A friend at work, Dana, helped me to realize that I needed to get out of the relationship. We were living together. I thought one day we would get married, but no, I've never been married and have never been asked."

After they had finished their meal, Michael paid the bill and they left. On the drive back they talked about their jobs and laughed about the day's events. When they arrived at Lisa's home, Michael escorted her to the door. When he kissed her, she welcomed it. They kissed a short time, and then Michael broke away. He smiled and said, "I think I better go now. I'll call you tomorrow."

"I look forward to it."

The next day Lisa got up early. She showered and dressed for church. As she walked into church, she immediately spotted Dana and her family. Lisa walked over to where they were seated. She hugged and kissed Dana and Maurice. Lisa spoke to the children. After the service, Dana invited her to come over for dinner. She accepted. When Lisa arrived home, she checked her cell phone. She saw that Michael had called. He left a message that he had to work, but if she wanted to do something later he would be home by five o'clock. She returned his call, but he did not answer. Lisa left a message saying, "I was invited to Dana's for dinner. It's at seven o'clock. I would love if you joined me. Please call me if you can make it."

She looked for an outfit to wear to Dana's. She picked a pair of navy blue pants with a white long-sleeved button-up top. The top complemented her body. She also chose a pair of navy blue three-inch heels. At five-thirty Michael called.

The phone rang. Lisa answered, "Hello."

"Hi, beautiful."

"Hi, Michael."

"I got your message. Are you sure Dana won't mind another guest?"

"I'm sure."

"Okay. I'll go. I'll pick you up at six thirty. Is that all right?"

"Yes. I'll see you then."

Michael arrived wearing grey slacks with a fitted shirt. It showed his well-muscular upper body. She blushed when he caught her looking at him. He greeted her with a light kiss on her lips.

He asked, "Are you ready?"

She said, "Yes."

They left and headed for Dana's home. Thirty minutes later they arrived at Dana's home. Michael opened the door for Lisa and helped her out of the car. They walked up the three steps of the house. Michael rang the bell. Dana opened the door. She hugged and kissed Lisa. Dana said while hugging and kissing Michael, "I'm happy to see you."

Michael said, "You don't mind?"

"Of course not."

They entered the house. Maurice came to greet them.

He said, "Hi Lisa." He kissed her.

Maurice put his hand out to Michael, saying, "Hey, man. Good to see you."

Dana said, "I'm just setting the table. Lisa, come in the kitchen. I have a few things to bring out."

Maurice said, "Come on, man, you can come have a seat."

Dana said, "Girl, I didn't know you were feeling him like that."

"He's a nice guy. Yesterday we went to the beach. We kissed for the first time."

"How was he?"

"Good. I like him Dana."

"Really? Ooh, you look like you've been bitten."

"Do I? I don't want to seem desperate."

"You don't. The fact that he's here speaks for itself."

The two brought the rest of the food out. Everyone sat down to eat; Dana sat Michael and Lisa next to each other. She occasionally looked at the couple and caught them staring into each other's eyes. Dana smiled at Maurice. She was happy for Lisa and Michael. After dinner the children disappeared and the couples went into the living room. They adults talked until eleven o'clock.

Lisa said, "I think we better be leaving. I have to work tomorrow."

Dana said, "We have to do this again."

For the next few months Lisa and Michael went out every weekend. Dana threw a New Year's Eve party. Ten minutes before midnight, Michael took Lisa out to the gazebo. He got on one knee and said, "Lisa, I love you. I've never wanted anyone as much as I want you. I've never waited for anyone before you. I want our time together to be special. Will you be my wife?"

Lisa was surprised. She looked at him to make sure that he meant what he said. She saw the truth in his eyes. Lisa said, "Yes."

He placed a two-carat platinum diamond ring on her finger. He got up, and they kissed at the stroke of midnight. When they stopped kissing, Michael said, "Happy New Year, beautiful."

He smoothed the side of her face with his hand.

Lisa said, "Happy New Year."

They sat out in the cool air for a while until Lisa shivered.

Michael said, "You're cold."

"Just a little."

"Come on, let's go in."

They returned to the house. Dana went and hugged Lisa and handed her a glass with champagne in it. She did the same to Michael.

She said, "Happy New Year."

They returned the greeting. At 2:00 a.m. everyone began to leave. Lisa and Michael remained until all the other guests had left. When the last guest had gone, Lisa held her left hand out and said, "We're engaged."

Dana looked down at the ring and said, "Congratulations." She hugged her friend. "I'm so happy for you."

When Michael and Maurice came out of the kitchen, Dana was smiling so broad that Michael said, "She told you."

Dana went up to Michael and hugged and kissed him.

Maurice smiled and said, "I guess so."

Dana scolded, "You knew and didn't tell me."

"Michael asked me not to."

"I can't believe you two."

Lisa said, "Well we better go."

They all said their good-byes. When Lisa and Michael got into his car, Lisa asked, "So when do you want to get married?"

"I don't think that we need to have a long engagement. How about next summer?"

"I thought about June. That will give us enough time to get things together."

"That sounds good. Do you want a big wedding?"

"Not really, but I want to get married in a church and I know a woman who owns a beautiful hall and bed and breakfast. It's called the Ward Reception and Bed and Breakfast. I would like to have our reception there. Michael, what are we going to do with our homes?"

"Well, I thought about that. Have you ever thought about selling your home?"

"Not really. I never thought that I would be getting married either."

"So you're not opposed to selling then?"

"No. What did you have in mind?"

"I thought we would both sell our homes and buy a larger place to raise a family. Where would you like to live?"

"Away from the city. I want to raise our children away from the fast pace of city life."

"I've been looking at Williamsburg. It's not very developed, and it's a nice area. I can take you up to see it whenever you like."

"You've really been thinking about this."

"Yes I have. You've been on my mind ever since our first dance at Dana's party."

The two made plans to go to Williamsburg to look around. Lisa called Dana and asked her to be her matron of honor. She then called Sara an asked her to be her bridesmaid. Michael asked Maurice to be his best man.

The women met at the mall. Lisa, Sara, and Dana shopped for dresses. Dana helped Lisa with all of her wedding plans. As the months got closer, Lisa decided to put her house up for sale. She and Michael decided to have their home built and live in his home while they waited for it to be completed. The night before the wedding, Lisa hung out with Dana. Dana threw her a bridal shower. After the shower, Lisa confided in Dana that she was worried about her wedding night.

Dana said, "I was a little nervous on my wedding night."

"Even though you had been with each other?"

"Yes."

"I think that I wouldn't be as nervous if we had been together."

"What, you guys haven't made love?"

"No. Michael just started coming in my house since I put it on the market. He has been helping me get things together."

"Has he ever tried anything?"

"I've felt that he's wanted to when we're kissing, but I feel him pulling away. I'm kind of happy because even though we know it's not my first time, it will feel like it."

"I think that's nice. Are you planning to have children right away?"

"We've talked about that. You know I'm not getting any younger. We're not going to use birth control."

"How many children do you want to have?"

"Four."

"Well if you ever need a babysitter, I'm available."

"Good."

With that they got quiet and soon drifted off to sleep. The next morning they awakened and began getting ready for the wedding. Sara came over to get dressed. The flower girls and ring bearer came half a half hour before the limo. After everyone was dressed, they entered the limo and headed to the church. As they pulled up to the church, the wedding party got ready to exit the limo. The limo pulled up to the curb. The driver exited the limo and opened the door for the wedding party. The flower girls exited first. Once they entered the church, they began to drop rose and lily petals. The ring bearer followed next, and then the bridesmaid. Dana kissed Lisa and said, "See you inside." She began her walk. Once she had made it to the front of the church, everyone was instructed to stand. The organist began to play, and the singer began to sing, "You and I." Lisa was helped out of the car by Dana's son and escorted to the front of the church. When they reached the last pew, Michael met her. Alex placed her hand in Michael's. The minister began, "We are gathered here today to witness a most memorable occasion—two people coming together and leaving as one. Michael and Lisa have written their own vows. Michael, you may begin."

Michael began, "Lisa I knew from the moment I met you at Dana's that you were special. From that first dance I couldn't get you off my mind. I knew that you were meant to be my wife. I promise to love, honor, cherish, and put you before all others until death do us part."

The minister said, "Lisa."

Lisa began, "Michael, something in me awakened when I met you. I was blessed the night that I met you, and I am blessed to be standing here today beside you. I love you more than I can say, and I hope by me saying that I'll always love you, honor you, and cherish you until death do us part will show you just a small measure of my devotion."

The minister said, "Michael and Lisa have expressed their love and commitment to each other. Who gives this woman?"

Alex stood up and said, "I do."

Michael placed the ring on his bride's finger. Lisa placed the ring on Michael's finger.

"Is there any reason these two should not be wed?"

The minister paused a minute. No one said anything. He continued, "I now pronounce you husband and wife. You may kiss your bride.

Michael took Lisa into his arms, and they kissed.

The minister said, "I would like to present Mr. and Mrs. Charles."

Everyone stood up and clapped. The couple left the church. Everyone exited the church. They headed to the reception. When the wedding party entered the hall, each couple was introduced. The bride and groom had their first dance. After a few minutes, the wedding party joined them. After the dance, everyone sat down for dinner. Once dinner was served and eaten, dance music was played. The couple walked around thanking their guests for coming. After the reception was over, the couple stayed over in the bed and breakfast because their flight wasn't until the next morning. On the wedding night, they walked down to their room. Michael put the key card into the door. He pushed the door open. Before entering the room, Michael picked Lisa up and carried her into the room. Once in the room, he closed the door and began to kiss her. He kissed her gently on her lips, on her forehead, on her nose, and then on her neck. She held the back of his head. He moved back to her lips. After some time of kissing, he placed her on the bed. The room was decorated with white roses and lilies, champagne, and strawberries, and heart-shaped chocolate was placed on the night stand. The bed had red roses spread over the covers. Lisa took her head piece off.

Lisa said, "Wait here. I'll be back."

She went into the bathroom. While she was in the bathroom Michael poured them champagne. He placed some of the strawberries in the champagne. He pulled back the covers and placed some of the petals inside the covers. Lisa took a shower, dried off, and then sprayed perfume all over her body. She put on one of the negligies she received from the bridal shower. It was white, see through, and opened in the front. It was also *trimmed in satin.* It had a satin thong that was see through and trimmed in lace. She put on lotion that had a slight fruity flavor all over her body. When she exited the bathroom, Michael's eyes lighted up and then filled with desire as his eyes went over her body.

He said, "Why, Mrs. Charles—boy that sounds good—what are you trying to do to me?"

"You like?"

"Yes, wait here." He kissed her lightly on the lips and then went into the bathroom. He took a shower. When he came out, he was wrapped in a towel around his waist. Lisa became aroused. She had never seen him this exposed; Michael was well built but not bulky. Each muscle was well defined, and he had a six pack. Michael had a small waist line. As she looked him over, he smiled with pleasure. Michael walked over to the glasses of champagne and handed her one of the flutes.

Before they drank, Michael said, "To us."

Michael and Lisa toasted and then drank some of the liquid. Michael took Lisa's glass and then placed both of them on the night stand. Michael turned back to her, took her hands in his, and kissed them. He pulled her to him, and they began to kiss. Michael kissed Lisa's neck. He pulled back and said, "Ooh sweet. Does the rest of you taste like this?"

Lisa smiled. He continued to kiss and tease her body until neither one could take being apart. Michael took off his towel, revealing his arousal. Lisa was pleased. Michael leaned her back. Knowing that she had not been with a man in a long time, Michael was very gentle. He took his time, wanting to make sure Lisa felt as much pleasure as he.

The next morning they awakened and dressed reluctantly. They checked out of their room and headed for the airport. When they arrived at the airport, they checked their baggage and were soon allowed to enter the plane. They were in first class. Michael and Lisa fell asleep soon after boarding. The two held onto each other. When they arrived in San Francisco, the couple exited the plane and headed to baggage claim. When they retrieved their baggage, the couple went out to get the limo that was waiting for them. The couple was taken to their hotel.

When they arrived, Lisa said, "This is beautiful. I've heard of the Ritz-Carlton, but that was an understatement. This is gorgeous." They went to check in.

The desk clerk greeted them and asked, "Can I help you?"

Michael answered, "Yes, Mr. and Mrs. Charles."

"Yes. Here you are. May I have your credit card and photo ID?"

Michael handed him the items. After the clerk recorded his information, he handed Michael his credit card and ID. He motioned to the bell man to take their luggage.

"Thank you, Mr. Dubois I hope you and Mrs. Charles have a pleasant stay. If we can do anything to make your stay more pleasurable, please let us know."

Michael said, "Thank you."

They followed the bell man to the presidential suite. When they entered the room, Lisa said, "This is nice."

After the bell man left, Michael pulled Lisa close to him, and they began to kiss. He picked her up and carried her into the bedroom.

He placed her on the bed and then accompanied her. He began to undress her. After he undressed her, she in turn undressed him. They made love for several hours. Afterward they drifted off to sleep. When they awakened, Michael asked, "Are you hungry?"

Lisa gave him a mischievous look.

Michael responded, "Are you serious?"

Lisa began to kiss him. All he could do was succumb to her advances.

Michael asked, "Are we going to go out of this room, or are they going to find us here starving and exhausted?"

"Well I'm full."

"I think you need more than just me."

"No I don't. But if you insist we can go out and get dinner."

"Let's eat here tonight, and then we'll go out on the town tomorrow."

"Sounds good."

They showered and hesitantly dressed. They chose to eat at the Terrace, which was located in the hotel. During their meal, they fed each other. After the meal, they took a short walk outside of the hotel and then returned to their room. They sat on the balcony and enjoyed each other's company. They looked out into the night, enjoying the scenery.

As it began to get late, Lisa ran water in the Jacuzzi. They sat in it for a while talking about the wedding and their future together. As it got later, they showered and went to bed. They caressed and savored each other's touch until their bodies erupted. They fell asleep holding one another.

The next morning they awakened at nine o'clock. The two laid together, holding each other. They kissed each other for a while and then hesitantly got up and showered together. They took turns washing each other. Every touch was sensual. They kissed as they continued to enjoy each other's body. After they finished showering, they dried each other off as they continued to caress each other's bodies.

They looked over the brochures in the room. The two decided to eat at a nearby restaurant. After they ate breakfast, they decided to take the motorized cable car extended city tour. The couple boarded the cable car, along with the other tourists. The tour guide began, "Welcome to San Francisco."

The guide continued, "It is the entertainment and movie capital of the world. Talking geography, it is the second-largest city in the United States by population and largest in square miles. What you see here is the Golden Gate. It stretches over forty-two hundred feet. It took more than four years to complete and cost thirty-five million dollars. The bridge opened to vehicular traffic on May 28, 1937, at noon, ahead of schedule, I might add, and under budget. The GGB held the record for longest main suspension span for twenty-seven years. The bridge's two towers rise seven hundred and forty-six feet, making them one hundred and ninety-one feet taller than the Washington Monument. The bridge has five lanes and crosses Golden Gate Strait, which is about four hundred feet or one hundred and thirty meters deep. This bridge can be crossed by cars, bike, or even on foot. At the south end of the bridge is Fort Point. It was designated a national historic monument October 16, 1970. Fort Point was built out of brick in 1853–1861. This was the beginning of the Civil War. The historic fort was used as a base of operations for building the GGB."

As they continued the tour, the couple traveled to Chinatown. The tour guide said, "Chinatown is the fastest way to visit Hong Kong's present and past. This residential area is the host to authentic markets and fantastic inexpensive restaurants, for those watching their pocket books. There is little to nonexistent parking, so consider talking a taxi or bus. Chinatown was established in the mid-1800s when there was a boom of Chinese immigration to the United States. During this time, Chinese immigrants flocked to the United States because of the social and political conditions in China. Many immigrants were drawn by the gold that was being discovered in San Francisco, but many laborers worked on the railroad system. During this time the bay came as far as Montgomery Street. This made the location of Chinatown the port of entry for the bulk of the Chinese immigrants. To cut down on the number immigrating, strict laws were created between the 1800s and early 1900s. This made it more difficult for Chinese immigrants. Only select immigrants were allowed in the United States. In the 1950 and '60s, the laws were repeated and this town began to grow again. The current look of Chinatown is not how it looked originally. The 1906 earthquake destroyed Chinatown, which was mostly made up of wooden shacks. They wanted to move Chinatown, but after much debate, it remained in its original location. The town was done over a lot to attract western tourists. Although the architecture is not true to Chinese architecture, the food, culture, and people remain to bring its authenticity to the area."

After their three-and-a-half-hour tour, they returned to their hotel. Michael ordered in, and they enjoyed their dinner by candlelight. They went for a walk and then returned to their room. They sat on the balcony.

As they looked over the city, Lisa marveled over the lighted hotels and restaurants. She thought, *How beautiful.* The city at night, even though it was a weekday, seemed to be as busy at night as in the daytime. Everyone, probably tourists, she thought, moved around the city, going in and out of shops, hotels, and cars. Michael got up from where he had been sitting next to Lisa; he bent down and kissed her on her lips.

He said, "I'll be right back."

He went into the bathroom and ran water in the Jacuzzi. He left the room and went to the gift shop. He purchased a dozen roses. He returned to their suite. He returned to the bathroom and took six of the roses and crumbled them into the water. He then took the roses off the stems and dropped the remaining roses into the water whole. He went back out to the balcony. Michael reached down and picked Lisa up. He carried her into the bathroom, where soft music was playing. He began to take her clothes off. Michael kissed her and then removed his clothes. He took her hand, and they entered the Jacuzzi together. He sat behind her. The sat quietly for a short time, and then he kissed her neck.

Lisa said, "What are you doing?"

"Kissing my wife."

"That sounds so nice."

She turned her head and kissed him on the lips. They kissed for some time, and then Michael lifted her into his arms and carried her out of the bathroom to their bed. They made love for hours before succumbing to exhaustion and fell asleep.

The next morning they awakened. Michael ordered room service. They ate and lounged during the day. By that night, Michael and Lisa decided to go out. They went out to Levende Lounge. They enjoyed the music and thought the food was excellent. Michael and Lisa returned to the hotel early. They lounged and just enjoyed each other. On Friday they visited the Japanese Tea Garden. As the two entered the garden, Lisa read, "The Japanese Tea Garden was first developed as the Japanese Village at the 1894 San Francisco midwinter International Exposition or the World's Fair, which was held in the area that is now the music concourse. The garden is the oldest public Japanese Garden in the United States." The couple walked through the garden, admiring the garden flowers and exhibits. As they continued to walk through the garden, she read about the Haggier family who lived in, maintained, and enhanced the Japanese Tea Garden from 1895 until 1942 and the beginning of World War II forced them to leave and relocate to concentration camps with other Americans of Japanese descent. Lisa thought, *How awful it must have been for the family to not only be taken to a concentration camp but to also have to leave this beautiful, mesmerizing place.*

After leaving the garden, they continued on to Alcatraz Island. The tour guide began, "Alcatraz Island, called Alcatraz and also known as the Rock, first served as a lighthouse, then a military fortification, then a military prison, followed by a federal prison until 1963. In 1972 it became a national recreation area. Today it is a historic site operated by the National Park Service as part of the Golden Gate National Recreation area. The first Spaniard to discover the island was Juan de Ayala in 1775. He charted San Francisco Bay and named the island La Isla de los Alcatraces, which traditionally translates to 'Island of the Pelicans.'" He showed a picture of the island between 1850 and '51.

He continued, "As far as the military history, the island's earliest recorded owner is Julian Workman, to whom the island was given by Mexican Governor Pio Pico in June 1846 with the understanding that a lighthouse would be built. It should be noted that Julian Workman is the baptismal name of William Workman, who was co-owner of Rancho La Puente and a personal friend of Pio Pico. The island was bought for $500 in the name of the United States government by John C. Fremont. The island was used to house Civil War prisoners as early as 1861. In 1898, during the Spanish American War, the population increased from twenty-six inmates to four hundred fifty. After the historical 1906 San Francisco earthquake, civilian prisoners were transferred here for safe confinement.

"By 1912, there was a large cell house, and by the 1920s a large three-story structure was nearly at full capacity. On October 12, 1933, it changed hands again. The United States Disciplinary Barracks on Alcatraz was acquired by the United States Department of Justice. The island became a federal prison in 1934. The prison in its twenty-nine years that it was open housed notables such as Al Capone, Robert Franklin Stroud, better known as the Birdman of

Alcatraz, James Bulger, known as Whitney, and Alvin Karpis. Also interesting is that Alcatraz housed for the Bureau of Prison Staff and their families. Although fourteen escapes were attempted, none were ever carried out. More information can be found in the museum. On March 21, 1963, the prison was permanently closed by decision of US Attorney General Robert F. Kennedy. It was closed because it was far more expensive to house prisoners than other prisons, $10 versus $3 per prisoner. The United States Penitentiary in Marion, Illinois, was opened the same year, which served as a replacement."

As they were winding down, the tour the guide said, "One more notable fact, in 1969 a group of Native Americans of many different tribes relocated to the bay area under the Federal Indian Reorganization Act of 1934 and occupied the island. They proposed an education, ecology, and cultural center. During their occupation, a fire broke out and many buildings were damaged. After the occupation, many of the buildings were destroyed by the federal government."

After leaving the island, the two talked about the tour. Lisa asked, "What did you think about the tour?"

Michael answered, "It was interesting. What did you think about the tour?"

"I enjoyed it. I especially enjoyed the gardens."

After the tour, they returned to the hotel and rested. By evening they got up, dressed, and went to LuLu's. They ate and then danced to a few songs. As it got later, they returned to the hotel. They talked about the day's events and decided to get one more tour in before leaving Saturday night. Saturday they woke up early and dressed. They went down to the hotel lobby. They went to Grace Cathedral. After touring the cathedral, they returned to their room. They ordered in while packing. By seven o'clock, they were on their way to the airport. After arriving at the airport, they checked in. The waited at the boarding gate for a half hour before being called for first-class boarding. When they boarded the plane, they sat back. Lisa snuggled close to Michael. He held her close with one hand. They drifted off to sleep once the plane took off. A few times they awakened. They snacked on wine and the small meal that was brought to them. Once they arrived in Newark, the plane landed. They retrieved their luggage and headed to pick up Michael's car. When they got in the car, Michael headed to his home. When they arrived, they exited the car. Before entering the house, Michael picked Lisa up. She placed her arms around his neck. They entered the house.

Lisa said, "This is nice."

Michael said, "Why, thank you, Mrs. Charles."

He put her down and showed her around the house.

Lisa said, "Are you sure you want to sell your home?"

"Exactly, my home. I want it to be our home."

"I could get used to this."

"We can have them work in some of these designs when they design the inside of our home in Williamsburg."

"I forgot about that."

"That's why you have me."

Michael checked the voicemail. There was a message from their realtor saying they had a buyer for Lisa's home.

Lisa said, "Great."

Lisa showered and decided to lay down. Michael looked through the mail. He showered afterward. When he came out of the bathroom, Lisa had fallen asleep. He pulled her close to him and held her as he fell asleep. The next morning when Michael awakened, Lisa had gotten up, showered, and gone into the kitchen and made breakfast. He smelled the aroma and followed it.

He said, "Hi, beautiful." He kissed her. "I see you're making yourself at home. Is everything ready?"

"No, the biscuits are still cooking and the bacon is just about done."

"I'm going to take quick shower and I'll be right back."

When he returned, she had set the table and was beginning to put the food on the table. He walked over to Lisa and took her into his arms.

He said, "This is nice."

He bent down and kissed her. They kissed a few minutes, and then she hesitantly stopped.

"Don't start anything. I want you to eat before it gets cold."

"Yes, Mrs. Charles."

"I love the way you say that."

"I love saying it."

They sat across from each other as they ate.

Michael said, "This is good. Mine never tasted this good. I did good. I got a beautiful woman who can cook."

Lisa said, "Thank you."

They finished their meal and cleaned up the kitchen. They decided to go to Lisa's house. When they arrived there, Lisa said, "This feels weird."

"What?"

"I miss my place. I can still remember when I closed on my house."

"Are you having second thoughts?"

"No. This is my past, and you are my future. I have a lot of memories of my place, but what we are about to embark on will give me better memories. I look forward to our house being built, us moving in, decorating, and raising a family with you."

"I never thought that I would be looking forward to having a family, but I am."

They went through the house. Her personal items had been placed in the garage. They rented a van the next day and removed them. They took them to Michael's house. They met with the prospective buyers a week later. Although her furniture was only a couple of years old, Lisa didn't want to take any of it with her. The couple that was buying the place were also newlyweds. They had one child. This was their first home, and they were moving from their parents' home. While looking at the house, they admired the furniture. Lisa offered to give it to them. They gladly accepted her offer. Everything went through. Lisa was happy she could give her furniture to someone rather than give it to Goodwill to sell.

A month later, Lisa called Dana. Dana answered the phone, "Hello."

"Hi."

"Hey, girl. How's things? How was your honeymoon?"

"Dana it was wonderful. I think that I love Michael even more."

"So then things went great."

"Yes. It was so nice. He is so romantic. I wasn't as nervous as I thought. He was such a gentleman."

"I'm so happy for you. You needed someone like Michael after that other one. Oh, by the way, they declared Sandy incompetent to stand trial. She was given a three-year sentence to a mental institution and three-year probation term."